GOODBYE, ENORMA

an Emmett Love Western - Volume 4
John Locke

TELEMACHUS PRESS

This book is a work of fiction. Names, characters, places and incidents are either the product of the author's imagination or are used fictitiously. Any resemblance to actual persons, living or dead, or to actual events or locales is entirely coincidental.

GOODBYE, ENORMA

The publisher does not have any control over and does not assume any responsibility for author or third-party websites or their content.

Cover designed by: Telemachus Press, LLC
Cover Art :
Copyright © shutterstock 115888612/Alan Poulson Photography
Copyright © istockphoto 21929821/bubaone

Published by: Telemachus Press, LLC
http://www.telemachuspress.com

Visit the author website:
http://www.donovancreed.com

ISBN: 978-1-939927-30-9 (eBook)
ISBN: 978-1-939927-31-6 (EPUB)
ISBN: 978-1-939927-32-3 (Paperback)

Printed in the United States of America

10 9 8 7 6 5 4 3 2 1

GOODBYE, ENORMA

PART ONE: BISCUITS AND BOOBS

CHAPTER 1

WATCHIN' GENTRY MOVE about the room is like eatin' sweet peaches from a can.

And it's not just me that thinks so. I reckon half the men in Kansas would give a days' wages for one a' her smiles.

She's standin' in front of me now, holdin' a basket of biscuits, sayin', "Can you drop this by the Stitz's when you go in to do your sheriffin' today?"

I was lookin' forward to biscuits for breakfast, but see none on my plate, so it seems logical to ask, "Are you givin' away *all* my biscuits?"

"Well, listen to you!" she says. "Didn't I spend all yesterday afternoon making four batches? And didn't you eat half a batch all by yourself, for dinner?"

"I'm right fond of your biscuits," I say.

She smiles.

1

"Thank you, Emmett. I know you worked through months of bad batches with hardly a complaint, which is one of the reasons I love you so much. But you know as well as I do the Stitzes have fallen on hard times."

"We been through this before. Harlan don't accept charity."

"I'll admit he's a proud man. But his family needs help."

"I'll try. But don't be surprised if he says no."

Gentry shakes her head. "Men!"

"Men? I was only talkin' about Harlan Stitz!"

"Don't go getting your dander up, Sheriff," she says, then winks, and goes back to her chores. The wink's a good sign. Means I'll have a warm bed tonight if I can find a way to make Harlan take the biscuits. I think on it a spell, then take a minute to think about dander.

All my life I heard people say, "Don't get your dander up!" To this day I got no idea what dander is, where it's located, or why a man shouldn't get it up. When I was a kid I thought dander was another word for pecker, 'cause my girl cousins used to say gettin' your pecker up only leads to trouble. Back in them days my mother never said the word pecker, but she was fond of sayin' dander. It come natural to think dander was a polite word for pecker.

But it ain't.

If it was, Gentry wouldn't talk about my pecker in one sentence, and my dander in another. She'd say pecker for both things.

I stare at the basket in my hand.

"What now?" Gentry says.

2

"This is a frilly way for the Dodge City Sheriff to make a house call."

"Don't be silly. You're Emmett Love. Who in this county would dare poke fun at you?"

"The Clantons, the whores, the Miller boys, Rafe Lawson, Bose Rennick..."

"Bose Rennick? Where'd that name come from? Bose hasn't been here in years."

I decide not to tell her I heard he was spotted in Kansas recently. A' course Kansas don't necessarily mean Dodge.

She says, "It's a proper church-type picnic basket."

"With a calico table cloth," I say. "And ribbons streamin' down the sides!"

"No one's going to make fun of you. The whole territory's scared to death of your jail cells. They're afraid you're going to lock them up indefinitely, since you put so much time and money into building them."

She's right. Lately the most vile men in the territory have come to town and surrendered their side arms without bein' asked! Instead of beatin' other people senseless, these same men have been seen helpin' little old ladies cross the streets. I swear, if I'd known a proper jail would have this effect, I'd a' built one long ago.

Gentry points at the picnic basket and says, "Maybe you'll be able to collect it on your way home tonight. And Emmett?"

I look at her.

"Be sure to ask after little Ben. He's been feeling poorly."

I give her a grin. "Got any messages for Enorma?"

She cocks her head. "Did you just say that to me? And are you honestly wearing that silly look on your face?"

She tosses her head like a sassy filly. "I guess I ought to be thankful the Sheriff of Dodge City has a peaceful enough town to let him concentrate his attention on a fourteen-year-old early bloomer."

"I just like her name is all."

"Is that what you men talk about when I'm not around? A fourteen-year-old girl's titties?"

"It ain't just the men. The whole town's in an uproar! Amanda Jeffries says they're a tourist attraction. And Reverend Murphy claims they're proof God ain't abandoned the town."

She pauses a minute, then says, "You made up that part about Reverend Murphy."

"I did indeed," I say, grinnin'.

"I suppose you'll be glancing at her this morning to see if they've grown since your last gawk."

"I'd rather gawk at yours," I say.

"Lift your eyes, wild man. You had your poke last night. I'll not have you staring at my chest while the air's still holding talk about Enorma's bosoms."

"Thing about Enorma, last fall, there weren't nothin' to notice. But in January, Silas Green rode past her and fell off his horse."

She frowns. "I'll admit she's blossomed beyond anything I've seen at any age. But Silas Green's a grown man!"

"It ain't just the bosoms," I say. "It's the name. Someone says the name, we can't help but laugh."

"And that never gets old?"

4

"Enorma Stitz?" I say. "Nope, never does."

She frowns again.

I say, "You still smile whenever I talk about what Alice Crapper's been up to."

She turns her head so I won't see her smile. Then says, "I used to smile at that poor woman's name when I was a teenager."

"You were a teenager last year. And anyway, I guess Alice couldn't help fallin' in love with a Crapper."

I peek around her shoulder and watch her mouth.

She fights it, but thinkin' about Alice is too much. She punches my arm playfully and says, "Stop it!"

Then she laughs.

"Guess you ain't so mature after all," I say. "And I'm right glad of it!"

She says, "Alice knew what she was getting herself into when she married Mr. Crapper. But poor Enorma was named for her grandmother, and no one could have foreseen her ma would lose her husband and wind up marryin' a Stitz."

"Enorma Stitz," I say.

I laugh.

"Nope, never gets old."

Gentry shakes her head. "Maybe I'll fetch the basket myself this evening."

"Suit yourself," I say, chucklin'.

She looks up at me.

"Why, Emmett Love!"

"What?"

"You steered this whole conversation about Enorma into making me jealous, so I'd fetch that basket myself to-night, instead of making you do it."

I give her a wink and head out the door carryin' my sissy basket of biscuits, hopin' not to run into Bose Rennick, a man so patently intolerant he once shot a man at a campfire for givin' up a bean fart.

CHAPTER 2

LESS THAN TEN feet into my journey, I hear the front door open behind me.

I turn to see Gentry starin' after me, like somethin's on her mind that was left unsaid.

"What's wrong?"

She motions me back inside. I follow her to the kitchen, set the basket on the table, take a seat. Gentry crosses the floor to our daughter's room, peeks her head through the half-open door a few seconds, then closes it. She walks quietly to the table, takes the seat closest to me, and whispers, "It's about Scarlett."

"What about her?"

"She was talking in her sleep again."

"I didn't hear her."

"Nor would I expect you to. You were snoring to keep the devil away."

"I do sleep well indoors."

"As you should. So I slept with Scarlett half the night."

I frown. "I'm sorry to hear that. I like wakin' up beside you."

"I like it, too, Emmett. The only reason I got up is I heard her say 'Yes, ma'am.'"

"She was practicin' her manners in her sleep?"

"That's what I thought at first, so I went to check, and found her sitting straight up in bed, eyes wide open, staring at the wall. But she was sound asleep."

"What else did she say?"

"Nothing I could understand. She was making all sorts of hissing sounds. She'd hiss, then stop a few seconds, like she was listening to someone. Then hissed some more. It was like a whole conversation."

"Did you try to wake her?"

"Of course! I climbed in her bed, put my arms around her, hugged her, tried to get her to lie down with me. But she was rigid as a tree trunk."

"You checked her head for fever?"

"I did. Her temperature was normal, and her clothes were dry. She wasn't sick, Emmett."

"What made her stop talking?"

"I guess she was done."

I try to puzzle it out in my head, but come up with nothin', 'cept to ask, "Did you check outside, to see if anyone was out there talkin' through the wall?"

"If someone was out there I would've heard."

I reckon that's true. My hearin's good, but Gentry can hear a bug blink.

Scarlett's door opens.

"Hey, sleepyhead!" I holler.

"Hi Papa. Hi Mama."

Gentry says, "How do you feel, sweetheart?"

Scarlett stares straight ahead, then blinks a couple of times and says, "I'm smarter now."

CHAPTER 3

"YOU'RE SMARTER THAN you were yesterday?"

"Yes, sir," Scarlett says.

"You've always been smart for three years old."

"Yes. But I'm smarter today."

Gentry and I look at each other, both thinkin' the same thing. She *does* sound smarter than she did last night. By a long shot. Like if you weren't lookin' at her, you might take her voice to be that of an eight-year-old's.

"Let's hear your calls," I say.

She licks her lips and whistles the sound of a white-throated sparrow.

If I'm stunned, Gentry's dumbstruck. Not because Scarlett knew the call, but because it was near perfect.

"That's my call," Scarlett says. "It means I'm safe."

"That's right. Now do your danger call."

She whistles like a cardinal.

"Best I ever heard from a three-year-old," I say, marvelin' at the change since yesterday. A' course, the sparrow and cardinal calls are about the easiest, most distinctive a child can make, so even though they're alarmin'ly good, it ain't like she's done somethin' witchy.

But then she *does* do somethin' witchy.

She makes my call.

Mine ain't easy. Took me years to perfect. And she just done it better than me.

"That's the wood warbler," she says. "That means you're near. Want me to make Mama's call?"

Before I can answer, she mimics the wood thrush.

"And this is Shrug's."

Shrug's call is the chipping sparrow, one of the hardest to make.

But she whistles it anyway.

"When did you learn all them calls?"

"I went to bed thinking of them, and woke up knowing them."

"You talk like an eight-year-old."

"That's 'cause I'm smarter now."

She whistles another call, and I feel the color drain from my face. Gentry crosses herself. Scarlett laughs like she's heard the funniest joke ever.

Terrified, Gentry says, "What's happening, Emmett? What kind of sound is that?"

"It's Rose's whistle. No one can make it."

"Why not?"

"It's two birds at the same time. A marsh wren and...well, I don't know the other one. But it's Rose's call. No doubt about it."

Gentry says, "Where did you hear that?"

"In my head."

Gentry looks at me. "I'm scared, Emmett. You've got to *do* something!"

I focus on what I just witnessed, then pat Gentry's hand. "It's a good thing."

"How can you possibly *say* that?"

"Rose is teachin' her things."

"Rose is a witch!"

"Shh! You don't mean that."

"I most certainly *do*! And *you* know it, too! Emmett, I was *with* Scarlett while this was happening last night. And Rose wasn't anywhere near. She's putting witchy voices in Scarlett's head! This is *not* a good thing. It's *sorcery!*"

"You know Rose is a good person. She's one of my two best friends in all the world."

"Then why is she doing this to Scarlett?"

"That, I don't know. But the secret things Rose knows are the most important things there are."

Gentry looks at Scarlett and says, "Where's Rose?"

Scarlett shrugs.

"Is she here in town?"

"No, ma'am. But she's on her way."

"Why?"

"She's going to watch me while you and Papa go on your trip."

"What trip?"

She shrugs.

I take a moment to wonder if Rose has changed any of the lessons we've taught Scarlett every day and night for the past year.

"Tell us what's bad," I say.

"Indians are bad."

"That's right. What else?"

"Outlaws."

"What else?"

"Strangers."

So far, so good. "What else?"

Scarlett gets a mischievous look on her face. Then says, "Cholera. Consumption. Brain Fever. Camp Fever. Typhoid. Scarlet Fever. Saint Vitas. Ulcers. Rubeola. Scurvy. Scrofula. Smallpox. Dropsy. Syphilis—"

"*Stop it!*" Gentry shouts. "*Oh, my God, Emmett! This is wrong! You need to tell Rose to stay out of our child's head!*"

"I'll do nothin' of the kind," I say. "I admit I don't understand half the things she just said, but what I *do* know is all them things are the kind of knowledge most people don't have. And there ain't nothin' in the world more valuable than knowledge."

Gentry knows it's true, but she's upset right now, like any young mother would be if she found out a witch was castin' spells in her daughter's head. But I'm not upset. I take it an honor that Rose chose Scarlett to learn these secrets of the world. That said, it would've been nice if Rose had thought to mention it to us ahead of time, or asked our permission.

While I'm thinkin' these thoughts, Gentry's goin' on and on about the evils of witchery. When she looks at me for support, I say, "I know you're upset about this, but—"

Gentry says, "Yesterday she knew what was bad and what was good. Good was Mama and Papa and Shrug. Good was minding your manners, sharing your toys, and being polite to grownups. Bad was strangers, Indians, outlaws, and snakes. Now, suddenly she's—"

Scarlett puts her hand up and says, "Snakes aren't bad, Mama."

Gentry whips her head around and looks at me with wide, frightened eyes. Then turns back to Scarlett and says, "You're wrong, honey. Don't you *ever* touch a snake! If you see a snake, back away and call us quick!"

Scarlett smiles. "Snakes aren't bad, Mama. They always, always, always..."

"Always what?"

"Obey."

CHAPTER 4

"WHAT ARE WE going to do, Emmett?"

"Scarlett said we're goin' on a trip together."

"So?"

"Well, I guess we ought to pack our bags."

"I don't understand you making light of this. It isn't funny! We've got a witch invading our daughter's head."

I give her a long hug, and feel her body shake and tremble. When we separate I dab the tears from her face and say, "You've always trusted me."

She bites her lip. "This is different. It's our daughter's *mind!*"

"How many times has Rose saved our lives?"

"That's not the point."

"It *is* the point. From all them years ago when she saved my arm from bein' cut off, to the trip where we brought you to Kansas, to the times she protected us from Bose Rennick, and David Wilkins and his men, Rose has been nothin' but a friend to this family. And if you tell me she's chosen to give our daughter the secret knowledge she's accumulated over her lifetime, well, that's a good thing."

Gentry thinks on it a long time. Then says, "Scarlett, would you like us to get her voice out of your head?"

"No, ma'am."

"Why not?"

"Rose is my friend. She's teaching me how to save the town."

"What do you mean?"

"She's teaching me sickness cures."

A look of concern crosses Gentry's face. "Is someone sick?"

"No, ma'am."

"But they will be soon?"

"Yes, ma'am."

"Who's going to get sick, honey?"

"Everyone."

"Everyone?"

She nods. "Unless we fix it. Can we go to the river today?"

"I was planning to bake biscuits."

"We should go to the riverbank."

"Why?"

"I need some snake shit."

Gentry does a double-take. "You *what?*"

"I need snake shit," Scarlett says. "And lots of it!"

I try not to smile.

Gentry says, "You will *not* use that sort of language in this house, young lady!"

"Yes, ma'am."

"*Ever again!*"

"Yes, ma'am."

"Tell her, Emmett."

"Don't say shit, honey. Not around your ma."

Gentry gives me a sour look, so I add, "Or in the house. You understand?"

"Yes, Papa."

Gentry frowns. "Don't say that word at all. Anywhere."

Scarlett looks at me.

I say, "Honey, if you want to play with snakes, you have to stop saying shit."

"*Emmett!*" Gentry says, scoldin' me.

"Sorry. I was just tryin' to be clear."

To Scarlett I say, "Where are me and mama goin'?"

"On your trip?"

"Uh huh."

"Philadelphia."

I almost say "no shit?" but think better of it just in time.

CHAPTER 5

MOST BEAUTIFUL WOMEN want you to think they're
smart, and most smart women want you to think they're
beautiful.

Gentry's both.

A'course, her learnin' ain't had time to catch up to her
beauty, now that she's grown into the prettiest woman I ever
saw. To her credit, Gentry don't rely on looks alone. She's
workin' hard to school herself in wifely ways, like cookin'
and chorin'.

Not that we're married (we ain't!)

And not that she wants me to propose marriage (she
don't!)

She claims our age difference is too great, and says she's
apt to fall in love with a young, handsome man, and says if
that happens she don't want to feel guilty about runnin' off.
A' course, them comments make me smile, 'cause the truth

is no woman in all of Kansas is more loyal and true than my Gentry.

The real reason Gentry don't want to marry me has nothin' to do with my age or looks. It's about them five years she spent workin' in brothels, where she saw a thousand miserable husbands takin' comfort with whores, and in saloons, where she saw another thousand spend night after night tryin' to drink their unhappy sorrows into smiles. Gentry don't want to be one a' them wives that cries herself to sleep every night from loneliness, boredom, or heart-break. She says if we live together outside marriage I'm more apt to find my happiness in *her* bed, and at *her* table, 'stead of elsewhere.

The bed part ain't a problem, and never was. But the kitchen?

If a man was to complain—which I ain't—he might say Gentry's ability to cook has lagged behind her determina-tion. After two hard months in the kitchen, she ain't passed the biscuits-and-bacon stage, and of the two, she's made more progress with the biscuits.

I always thought cookin' was one a' them things that came natural to women, like birthin' babies and changin' diapers. Of course, the day I said them words to Gentry I got a cold bed 'stead of a special smile, and learned right quick not to tell her about the things I thought came natural to women.

In any case, it weren't true, because what came natural to Gentry was to carve a two-inch-thick slice of bacon and warm it on a skillet, which made for tough chewin'. This went on till I figured a way to explain how I like my bacon in a manner that didn't invoke my ma or my grandma, and without makin' it sound like Gentry's way weren't the best of the bunch.

One thing that slowed her bacon-fryin' progress was my best friend, Shrug, who swooned over Gentry's two-inch-thick bacon. She still makes it thick and nearly raw for him, though it ain't particularly pleasant to watch him go after it on a plate.

But for me, Gentry's got the bacon down perfect, to the point Scarlett Rose calls it meat candy. And lately she's made progress on her biscuits to the point I ain't ashamed to offer 'em to needy families like the Stitzes, where I'm headed right now.

I'm walkin' 'stead of ridin' 'cause the stallion I'm least fondest of needs to be walked regular, since he don't like to be ridden in certain directions. This stallion belonged to my witchy friend, Rose, and either he's crazy, or she put a spell on him that only allows me to ride in a direction that leads to her. At one time he only led me to Gentry, but now that Gentry's with me I guess he wants to go home to Rose.

I can't blame him.

Rose is much better with horses than me, bein' as how she can talk to 'em. But Rose is livin' in Bowie County, by the Red River, and since Harlan's house is two blocks north of my place, I can't ride this particular horse to Harlan's. So I walk, and he follows at a distance of ten feet.

While walkin', I think about Harlan Stitz, who I met years ago, when he was a young ranch hand outside Maryville. Back in them days he claimed to have somethin' worth more than gold.

"What's that, Harlan?" I asked at the time. "A gold mine?"

"Nope."

"Treasure map?"

"Nope."

"Silver? Diamonds? Rubies? Spanish doubloons?"

"Nope."

This went on till he finally said, "A life plan."

"A what?"

"I got a plan for my life."

Harlan's plan was to stay out of trouble, save his money, start his own cattle ranch, find a proper woman, get married, have a mess a' kids, and live a happy life. His plan worked, to a point. He bought a small spread, spent three years buildin' his stock, but never managed to get the first herd to market.

See, Harlan's life plan didn't anticipate war breakin' out.

A couple years ago, on the way to Saint Jo, his herd got stole by Southern soldiers retreatin' from a hard-fought battle. On that occasion Harlan received a busted skull and a gunshot to the leg for protestin' the theft. The busted skull affected his speech such that he developed a stutter. Not only that, but his voice went up so high you'd think he was a three-year-old girl when he talks!

The day he got shot, Harlan dug the bullet out and dragged his leg eight miles to the Santa Fe Trail, where a widow named Mary Hammer happened to be drivin' the wagon closest to the spot where he collapsed in the dirt.

She and her kids stopped to give him food and comfort.

Mary patched him up best she could, and let him ride with her, plannin' to drop him off at his ranch north of Dodge. But when they got to his place they found his house burned to the ground. By then Harlan and Mary decided they had mutual needs. Her children, Ben and Enorma, had a mother, but no father, and Harlan had land, but no money. Mary had money, but no land.

Like I say, all this happened two years ago, when Ben was ten and healthy, and Enorma was twelve and normal-chested. After a long discussion, Harlan and Mary came to me with a new life plan. They agreed to marry and settle in Dodge if I'd take his sixty acres of land in trade for a plot on Main Street and title to the abandoned dry goods store in Old Dodge, twelve miles away.

I agreed.

Mary used her inheritance to build their house and rebuild the store in the town's current location. Things were lookin' up for the Stitzes till the supply wagons bringin' their stock from Saint Jo got robbed. Now they've got a finished, but empty store, and a house that ain't quite finished. Their dry goods store will eventually flourish, providin' they can get it stocked. In the meantime, the Stitzes have no garden to cultivate, no livestock to slaughter. They're on the verge of bein' rich, but till that happens, they're practically starvin'.

CHAPTER 6

"PICKLED PAR-ARR-ARRsley!" Harlan yells in his little girl's voice when he sees me headin' his way with my frilly basket.

"You may's well be wearin' bloo-ooo-OOOOmers and carryin' a daw-aw-OLLy!" he yells.

"Hey there, Harlan," I say. "Gentry's been practicin' her cookin', and made more biscuits than we can eat. She was hopin' Mary and the kids would give 'em a try and tell her if her cookin's up to snuff."

"That sounds like a fancy-ass way of offerin' us char-ar-ARRity!"

It'd be bad enough if Harlan's voice were only as high-pitched as a three-year-old girl's, but the busted skull gave him a stutter that makes his voice go even higher on certain words. It's powerful annoyin' to me, and even more so to my horse, who neighs loudly every time Harlan speaks. I can only imagine what Bose Rennick would do if he heard Harlan talk to him like this.

"It ain't charity," I say, "it's just Gentry, learnin' how to cook. If Mary's too busy to give an opinion I'll take 'em to Mavis Reynolds."

Harlan says, "Take 'em inside. Mary's a better cook than Ma-a-AAvis. She'll be able to hell-ell-ELLP Gentry."

My horse whinneys, and rears up. I calm him, tie him to the rail in front of Harlan's house, then stop to contemplate my actions. I'm a little skittish about goin' inside 'cause Gentry'll ask if I happened to see Enorma. I can't lie to Gentry, and don't *want* to see Enorma. Folks say one glance at her chest can turn a man into a pillar of salt.

I take a deep breath, enter the front door, place the basket on the table, and turn to make my getaway before Enorma's bosoms have time to enter my field of vision.

"Harlan?" Mary calls out.

"It's me, Mary. Emmett Love. Gentry had me bring over some biscuits."

Enorma suddenly appears in the doorway. "Hi, Sheriff!"

I spin around and try to get away so fast I slam my forehead into the door frame.

"Are you all right, Emmett?"

Did she just call me Emmett?

I look at the door, not her. Then blink a couple times and hope I didn't hit my head so hard my voice comes out like Harlan's. I try it out.

"Hi Enorma. Gentry sent biscuits."

"Oh, that's wonderful! Please thank Miss Gentry for me!"

She spies the basket and giggles. "You carried that frilly thing through town just now?"

"I did."

She giggles some more.

Still starin' at the kitchen door I say, "How's Ben holdin' up?"

"He's better today."

"Gentry'll be pleased to hear that."

We're quiet till Enorma says, "Umm...Can I get you somethin' Sheriff?"

"I'm good," I say.

"Well, okay then..."

She pauses a moment, then walks over, takes my hand, and leads me to the door like I'm some dim-witted man who forgot whose home he's in. I notice she's wearin' some sort of garment her ma must've made from a giant sheet. It don't show details, thank the Lord, but if you can picture two slaughter-sized razorbacks trapped in a sheet, fightin' to bust free, you'll have an idea what I'm tryin' not to see.

Someday Enorma Stitz'll have the healthiest, fattest babies west of the Mississippi. But for the time bein', her bosoms are blockin' my exit path.

"Thanks again, Sheriff," she says, holdin' the door open.

"Uh. Well, okay, then," I say, tryin' to edge my way past the considerable obstacles.

The flat truth is there ain't no graceful way to pass through the door without obtainin' intimate knowledge of the young lady's physicality. And I don't want to embarrass her by askin' her to take five giant steps back.

"Enorma!" Harlan shouts from the front yard. "Can't you see your tit-it-ITS are in the way? Back up so the poor man can pa-aa-AASSS through the door!"

"Oh! Oh *my*!" Enorma yells, and runs back to the bedroom, mortified.

"Sorry Sheriff," Harlan says.

"Much obliged," I say, and walk to where he's standin'. He says, "You ever seen tits like that on a mamm-amm-AMMAL?"

I shake my head. "Does it fluster you she's built like that?"

"The har-ar-ARD part's pretendin' not to no-oh-OTICE 'em."

I nod.

He says, "Could you ignore a Moo-ooo-OOOSE in your parlor?"

"I couldn't'," I say, "and I'm the right man to ask, since I keep a bear in my saloon."

"Well, thanks for not star-air-AIRIN' too much."

"I don't think of Enorma that way."

"Others do."

I 'spect he's right. At fourteen, Enorma's already two years past the age of consent, and bein' talked about all up and down the Santa Fe Trail. Cowboys come to town on Friday nights and ask the locals, "Is it true? Is there a girl in town named Enormous Tits?"

"Enorma Stitz," they say.

"Ain't that what I just said?" they ask. "Where *is* she? You ever *seen* 'em? How big *are* they?"

I feel bad for her. And Mary, Ben, and Harlan.

Especially Harlan.

His life plan seemed like a good idea at the time. Now it's left him broke, with a gimpy leg, an uncommon hatred of soldiers, and a funny way a' talkin'.

I get my horse and head to the *Spur* and see somethin' I never saw before: a dozen Indians walkin' their horses right down the middle of Main Street!

CHAPTER 7

I DRAW MY pistol, but Silas Green shouts, "It's okay, Sheriff! They're just here to talk."

Silas, Indian Agent, is ridin' alongside 'em. I notice they're wearin' warpaint, but that might be for show. In case it ain't, I keep my firearm outside the holster, and watch 'em pull their mounts to a stop twenty paces away.

"You should know better, Silas. I can't protect these Indians from the town. Someone's liable to get shot."

"Will you ride with us west of town so we can talk?"

I don't want Silas and the Indians to know I own a horse that won't ride westward, so I say, "East or south of town would be safer."

Silas hollers some Indian words, and them that understand him seem confused as to why east or south would be safer. But they're agreeable, so I mount my stallion and head south. We manage to get out of town without drawin' fire, though most of the town's men and boys are armed and followin' at a distance.

After a few minutes me and Silas dismount near an outcroppin' of rocks. The Indians remain on their horses. Several young warriors keep a wary eye on the townspeople, sixty feet away. I wave to show everyone I'm okay, and motion 'em to stop where they are. The experienced warriors seem more fidgety than I'd expect.

"What's got 'em spooked?" I say.

"The Grasshopper."

Silas is referrin' to my best friend, Shrug.

I don't blame 'em, for Shrug's a relentless Indian killer. Most area tribes call him by whatever word means *Grasshopper* in their language, 'cause Shrug can leap and jump great distances, and his deformed body goes more sideways than up-and-down. This, due to him havin' been trampled in a stampede at a young age. On that occasion every bone in his body was broken in one or more places. When the bones healed, he took on the shape and form of a wide stack of sticks. When he ain't leapin' and boundin' he walks like a crab and runs like a deer, 'cept that deer make noise when they cover ground, and Shrug don't.

A' course, Shrug can't ride a horse, or eat or drink normal, or hold a rifle, or fire one, for that matter, all of which might make you wonder why the Indians fear him so much. The reason is Shrug's an uncommon rock thrower. He's so accomplished I've actually seen him kill a runnin' deer with a single throw.

"Is he nearby?" Silas says.

"He's always nearby."

Shrug carries all sorts of special rocks in a sack around his waist. Some are heavy skull-thumpers that'll kill a man on impact. Others are sharp as knives. He chunks the heavy ones in a normal way and flings the sharp ones vertically.

It's them vertical throws that made him a legend among the Indians.

All tribes within a hundred miles tell the story of how one mornin' a warrior was takin' a piss when his pecker suddenly disappeared. It was a quiet mornin', and none of the other braves saw or heard a thing till the pissin' warrior started howlin' and makin' all the sounds you'd expect to hear when a man gets his pecker sliced off. They found the pecker and rock, and reasoned out what happened. They'd been huntin' Shrug from a distance for two days and had already seen him throw a rock and sever a rattlesnake's head. They watched him wrap the snake's body around his neck and eat it while racin' across the plains. These sorts of things like snake heads and peckers bein' sliced off by rocks'll spread terror through an Indian camp faster than smallpox, and make every brave think twice before pissin' in the open.

These days, accordin' to buffalo hunters, Indians throughout Kansas and Nebraska piss under blankets, just to be safe. A' course, if Shrug wanted to kill an Indian who's pissin' under a blanket, he'd just chunk a heavy rock at his head.

"How much do you know about these Indians?" Silas says.

"Not much," I say. "Nor do I speak their language."

"Most of these don't speak the same language, either," he says. "They're what's left of three tribes that were ravaged by soldiers. They joined up together, hopin' to survive."

I look at 'em. Some are Cheyenne, and others are dressed like whites. The rest are shirtless, with moccasins and white men's hats and pants.

"What do they want?"

"To live peacefully."

"Who's stoppin' 'em?"

"*Seriously*, Emmett? *Everyone! Everyone's* stoppin' 'em."

"I ain't."

"Maybe not, but *they* have no way of knowin' how long the town's gonna leave 'em be. Not to mention Shrug's got 'em scared shitless."

"You know damn well Shrug never killed any Indian, nor cut off his pecker, that weren't tryin' to catch or kill him first!"

Silas says, "Try not to sound so angry. You're agitatin' the chiefs." He motions them to relax. Then says, "I'll tell 'em you said the grasshopper only attacks in self-defense. That might give 'em comfort. But it ain't the reason we're here. They want me to discuss two things with you."

As he says that I notice a fat prairie moth flyin' toward us, lopsided, strugglin' to keep its dust-heavy wings airborne. Shrug considers these nasty bugs a delicacy. This particular one seems exhausted from the effort it took to fly here from wherever it came. It finally gives up and lights on a nearby rock. Shrug says moths cough when they land on hot rocks, and claims he can hear 'em do so. That could be a yarn, since I never heard one cough, and this one didn't, either.

31

Far as I know.

Then again, I wouldn't a' believed a man could throw a rock and slice off an Indian's pecker till the first time I saw Shrug toss one in my skillet. I cussed him loud and flipped it forty feet away. Shrug caught it 'fore it hit the ground, fetched it back, and roasted it on a stick. Since then I've only known him to eat pecker a time or two, but I still won't let him fry it in my pan.

I look at Silas and say, "What are the two things they want to talk about?"

"You know Jackson Corn, the trader?"

"Nope."

"He trades just past the Kansas border, near Rocky Bend."

"What about him?"

"He's a thorn in my side. I got no jurisdiction over his activities."

"What's wrong with tradin'? It's a noble profession."

"He's tradin' whiskey to the Indians for buffalo hides."

"How's that work?"

"He trades a gallon of Pine Top for a buffalo hide."

"What's he pay for Pine Top?"

"Sixty cents."

"And buffalo hides are sellin' for?"

"Eight-fifty."

"No shit?"

"Those are the true dynamics of the deal."

"The what?"

"The dynamics. That's what Washington calls it."

"Sounds like a helluva business."

"Well..."

I take my hat off, run my fingers through my hair. "You think Mr. Corn might be interested in sellin' his tradin' business?"

Silas frowns. "The chiefs want you to shut *down* his tradin' business."

I shove my hat back on. "Shut it *down*? That's the craziest thing I ever heard! Is he *forcin'* 'em to buy whiskey?"

"No, but the young braves can't help themselves. They keep sneakin' off to get it."

"Are the chiefs upset they're *payin'* too much? Maybe they'd rather work a deal with me. We sell top-grade whiskey at the *Spur*."

"You're missin' the point, Emmett."

"Which is what?"

"Indians have a natural disposition to drunkenness, such that eight ounces of whisky makes 'em crazy, and twice that makes 'em shoot each other."

"The chiefs can't stop the bucks from goin' to Corn's tradin' post?"

"No. And they've tried everythin' to stop 'em. When they started guardin' the buffalo hides the braves took to stealin' horses from their own tribe. With no hides to trade, they started tradin' *horses* for liquor! The chiefs are at their wits' end."

"Wait a minute. Ain't these the very chiefs that taught their braves to steal horses in the first place?"

"A' course. But they don't condone stealin' from their own *tribe!*"

"You're tellin' me these young braves get drunk and steal from their own people?"

"They do."

"Maybe we should send 'em to Washington to be politicians."

"This ain't a jokin' matter, Emmett. These warriors are fixin' to kill Jackson Corn and his partners."

"When?"

"Today."

"Well, that'd start a war!"

"Exactly what I told 'em, which is why I talked 'em into lettin' me have this meetin'."

I motion to the Indians. "Why'd *they* come?"

"They want to know if you plan to shut Jackson down."

"And if I don't?"

"They'll go straight there and kill him and his partners."

I think about what Silas calls the dynamics of the deal. Then say, "Seems like a helluva business Jackson Corn's put together."

"But you can see its wrong, can't you?"

"Decidin' what's wrong about it'd be easier if I didn't own a saloon. You might as well tell me the chiefs don't endorse whorin'!"

"Well, they don't."

"*What?*"

I shake my head. "How do you expect me to trust men who'd condemn whorin'?"

Silas says, "Try to focus on the Indian war for the time bein'."

"Well, I don't want a war this close to Dodge," I say, "And don't want them young bucks tryin' to steal the few horses we still have in Dodge."

"So you'll shut down Jackson Corn's business?"

"If I do, he'll just set up somewhere else. Or some other traders will."

He winks. "Would you consider lockin' 'em up? You know, for their own safety?"

"How many are there?"

"Six or eight."

Like everyone else in the county, Silas knows I've been itchin' to try out my new floor-to-ceilin' iron bar jail cells. Though I finished buildin' 'em a month ago I ain't managed to arrest the first person yet. Some are afraid the locks won't work and they'll get stuck and die in there, and others know Gentry's cookin' is legendary bad, and fear them are the vittles they'll be served while incarcerated.

I say, "It's appealin' to think a' tossin' six or eight men into my new jail cells, but I can't fault Jackson Corn for what he's doin'. I s'pect his trades ain't exclusive to Indians, and you say he ain't forcin' 'em to trade. It don't seem right to lock Corn up for earnin' a livin'.'"

I look at the Indians.

They look at me.

CHAPTER 8

"THEY'RE ITCHIN' TO massacre Jackson Corn and his partners," Silas says.

"Tell 'em I'll ride out and talk to Jackson. But just so you know, I'm not gonna lock people up for operatin' an honest business."

"What will you tell him?"

"That he can't trade whiskey to the Indians."

"And if he does?"

"I'll kill him."

"*Kill* him?"

"I ain't got room in my jail cells for everyone who wants to trade whiskey to Indians. It'd be easier to kill Corn and his partners. That ought to discourage others from doin' it."

"Well, Washington might not like that, but I think it'll please the Indians."

"It'll please 'em less when they hear the rest of my plan."

"What's that?"

"I aim to kill any Indian who tries to trade for whiskey."

"*What?*"

"Seems only fair."

"You're *insane!* They'll *never* go for that!"

"Tell 'em that's how it's gonna work."

He scowls.

I ask, "What's the other issue you wanted to discuss?"

He pauses a moment. Then says, "They want to buy Harlan Stitz's daughter."

"That ain't gonna happen."

"They're prepared to make a fair offer."

"Tell 'em she ain't for sale."

He frowns. "*That's* not gonna sit well."

"I don't give a shit *how* it sits! And I'll tell you somethin' else. These Indians are startin' to piss me off."

"It's part of their lore."

I give him a frosty look. "I don't even know what that means."

"All tribes tell a story that's been handed down for generations about a young woman whose bosoms were so large she fed the whole tribe durin' the winter to end all winters. Accordin' to tribal legend, she's Teats of Glory, the goddess of fertility."

"That sounds like a load of horse shit."

"I'm serious, Emmett. Her milk was said to be magical. It gave strength to the warriors. Made them indestructible. Her tits restored the tribes to their glory days."

John Locke

"Well, that's about the stupidest story I ever heard."

"It's what they believe, Emmett. It's their ancient, sacred story."

"Seems to me every time an Indian wants somethin', a sacred legend pops up."

"They're very sincere about this legend, Emmett. It only seems reasonable we should tolerate their beliefs."

"Their beliefs sound awful convenient to me. I guess they could make up *any* story and tell you it's part of their lore. You need to tell this bunch to find their own big-titted woman."

"They were tryin' to be nice about it, Sheriff. They were hopin' to offer up a fair trade. Now they'll probably just steal her."

I study the chiefs a minute. "They don't want their young-uns to trade for whiskey, but they'll trade for a *girl?* And even though they can't control their *own* young-uns, they're willin' to steal someone *else's?*"

"She ain't a young-un, Emmett. She's fourteen."

"Regardless, she belongs to her parents and the town of Dodge City."

"What's that supposed to mean?"

"Means I'll kill any Indian who tries to steal Enorma."

He gives me a careful look. "There's only one a' you, and close to fifty braves in their combined tribes."

"So?"

"If they decide to take Enorma, or kill Jackson Corn, I reckon there's not much you'll be able to do about it."

I give him a look of my own. "Is that a threat?"

"It's a statement of fact."

38

"I've got Shrug on my side, and the townspeople, if need be."

"It still ain't enough men to stop fifty braves."

"It's more than enough. It's guns and rifles against spears and arrows."

"Case you didn't notice, they've got plenty of guns."

"Their guns ain't reliable. And even if they are, they ain't got ammo. And even if they do, they can't shoot straight in the first place."

"What makes you think that?"

"They ain't got the proper equipment to keep their guns cleaned and oiled, nor enough ammo to practice shootin'. I can't tell you how many times I've killed three or more Indians without takin' a single hit."

He says, "When can you meet with Jackson Corn?"

"Soon as I get to my place and saddle a proper horse."

"What's wrong with this one?"

"Don't ask."

A stone suddenly explodes against the large rock, killin' the prairie moth.

The Indians scream their words for *grasshopper* and look around fearfully, while covering their crotches with their free hands.

At that moment, back in town, a woman screams.

The Indians turn their horses and begin a fierce gallop northward. I know what they're up to. They're gonna circle the town and come back in from the north entrance.

I jump to my feet and yell, "Guard the town!" As the town's men run to do it, I jump on my horse, kick his ribs, and...he promptly throws me ass over heels to the ground.

"*Damn you!*" I yell, shakin' my fist at him. I jump up to kick him, but he sidesteps me, so I reach for Silas's reins. He resists, so I punch his face. As he falls to the ground, he loses his grip and I snatch his reins, jump on his horse, and gallop toward town. As I pass the menfolk, I hear a horse bearin' down on me from behind.

I don't even bother to turn. I already know it's my own worthless stallion, keepin' a steady pace ten feet behind me.

Out the corner of my eye I see Shrug boundin' toward town from the east, and figure we'll get to the center of Dodge about the same time as the Indians. While gallopin' I can't help but wonder why the chiefs didn't try to kill me a minute ago when they had the chance, 'stead of turnin' this whole thing into a Dodge City street battle.

Within' a minute me and the Indians are on opposite ends of town, bearin' down on each other. Suddenly, they stop, so I do the same. Now we're a hundred yards apart, and I don't see Shrug, which is a good sign. Means he got here first, and is already on one of the rooftops, ready to fling rocks.

I instinctively reach for my rifle, but then it dawns on me I'm on Silas's horse, and he ain't got a rifle nor scabbard. It's just me and my sidearm and Shrug and his rocks, 'cause the town's men ain't arrived yet. I turn around in my saddle and see my horse. I call him, but he don't approach. I look back at the Indians and notice they ain't even lookin' in my direction.

They're starin' at somethin' on the ground, in front of Harlan Stitz's house.

I ride closer till I see it, too.

40

Then it hits me. This bunch of chiefs and warriors were distractin' us while two other braves snuck into town to steal Enorma.

But things didn't turn out the way they planned.

CHAPTER 9

THREE PEOPLE ARE lyin' facedown in Harlan's yard.

One of 'em's Harlan, but he's alive. The other two are Indians, but they ain't.

Alive, that is.

The two skull-crusher rocks beside the bodies tell me what I need to know about who killed the Indians.

But what happened to Harlan?

He rolls over, works his way to a sittin' position. Then blinks a few times, and looks at Mary and Enorma. Then says, "Don't worry about me. I'll be fine."

All three of 'em pause a minute, then start screamin'.

They're screamin' 'cause Harlan's voice has gone back to bein' normal!

I walk Silas's horse closer and motion the Indians to take their dead. We go through one a' them moments where we all know what everyone else is thinkin'. The chiefs and

42

warriors have lost two braves and wonder if they should avenge their dead by attackin' the town. But their braves are transfixed on Enorma, and aren't of a mind to take their eyes off her.

I yell, "Enorma! Go back in the house!"

She does.

By then, the men and boys are comin' up behind me pretty quick. I hold up my left hand to keep 'em from firin', while usin' my right hand to draw my gun so fast the Indians don't have time to twitch. By the time their eyes bug out, I've already spun my gun two full turns and holstered it. While they're tryin' to figure out what I just done, Shrug starts jumpin' up and down on a nearby roof, and I reckon the Indians come to the quick conclusion that two dead Indians is better than twelve peckerless ones.

Four braves dismount, collect the dead warrior's horses, and tie their dead to 'em. When they finally leave town, me and the town folk gather 'round Harlan, and he explains how the Indians showed up out of nowhere, plannin' to ambush him.

"Shrug killed 'em with two stones!" Harlan says, enjoyin' the sound of his normal voice.

"How'd you get that lump on your head?" I ask.

"One of the stones bounced off the Indian's skull and hit me so hard it knocked me out."

I look up at the rooftop where Shrug had been, but he's gone. He probably ran back to the rock to eat his prairie moth. I figure he killed the Indians, knocked Harlan out by accident, then ran to within a stone's throw of where me, Silas, and the Indians were, so he could protect me. A couple minutes later, Enorma or Mary must've come out-side, saw Harlan lyin' on the ground between two dead Indians, and started screamin'.

Before long Silas shows up. He's upset with me, but I'm more upset with him for helpin' the Indians create a diver-sion to steal Enorma. He claims he knows nothin' about that, and after hearin' him out I give him the benefit of the doubt, and return his horse.

While Harlan continues tellin' his tale, I walk my horse back to his stall. He's a beautiful stallion, but worthless un-less I need to find Rose. Since Rose is even better in an emergency than Shrug, I keep the stallion for that purpose, and exercise him regularly, by lettin' him follow me around town.

But he does vex the shit out of me.

Gentry says he'd be more agreeable if I'd give him a name, but I don't want an agreeable horse, I want a practical one, like the mustang in the adjoinin' stall that took me three months to break. That one's got a name. But I ain't about to name a horse I can't ride in all directions.

After puttin' my horse up, me, Harlan, and the men head to *The Lucky Spur* to celebrate Harlan gettin' his normal voice back.

"Harlan, your whole life is gonna change for the better!" our whore, Emma says, while winkin' and fondlin' her breasts. The wink's meant for Harlan, but the breast fondlin' is part of her nature, somethin' she does absent-mindedly when talkin'. Emma don't just *touch* her bosoms durin' con-versations, she gives 'em a real workout. If Enorma devel-oped that habit she'd need all day and some outside help to complete a full fondle. A' course, Emma's bosoms are plenty stout in their own right, and while her manner of gropin' in public is disconcertin' to most folks, I've noticed men seem to be more tolerant of it than women.

After two rounds of drinks the men take up a collection to get Harlan laid, but out of the whole bunch they only offer up three dollars and change. Gentry and I charge six dollars to poke our whores, but this bein' a special occasion, I offer him Leah, and tell her she can keep the full amount. Leah's an enthusiastic whore, but gets the fewest customers, due to a horrific facial scar, and because she's skinny as an orphan's cat.

As Leah and Harlan go upstairs, the men hooray him loudly. But when he comes back down a half-hour later, he's cryin' real tears.

Leah's cryin' too.

As it turns out, they were havin' a great time till Harlan's head hit the bedpost in such a way that his stammerin', little girl's voice came back just as bad as it had been before Shrug hit him with the rock.

Now that we know what causes his stammer to come and go, we take turns punchin' his head till he gets knocked cold. But when he comes to, he's still got that awful speech problem, and some cuts and bruises to boot.

"I ha-a-ATE to go ho-oh OHM," Harlan stammers. "How'm I gonna expla-ai-AIN this to Mar-air-AIRY?"

"Tell Mary the cure was temporary. And the rest of us won't talk about it, okay?"

They all agree, though I know the whores will let it slip, eventually.

They're a gossipy bunch.

Everyone watches Harlan head sadly back home, and I ask for volunteers to guard his house in case the Indians try to steal Enorma again. Some of 'em make undignified comments about how they'd be glad to protect Enorma, and how they'd go about it. I let that loose talk continue till their drink money runs out, then I ask how they'd feel if Enorma was *their* daughter? That question produces even worse comments, so I tell 'em if I hear any more loose talk about Enorma I'll put the men who said it in jail.

Everyone apologizes, inlcudin' them that didn't say nothin' bad in the first place, which leads me to wonder if I'll ever be able to jail my neighbors.

When the last man leaves I walk to my stable and saddle the one horse I can count on to take me wherever I want to go.

My mustang, Sally.

All she wants to do is ride around.

CHAPTER 10

MEETIN' JACKSON CORN turns out to be nothin' like I expected.

For one thing, he's dead.

At least that's what Sadie Nickers says, before askin' if I ever done it with a mule skinner.

I ain't.

I tell her every mule skinner I ever met was a man.

"So?" she says.

We're sittin' on stools by a long wooden table covered with buffalo hides. Besides Sadie, I count five: four men, and an uncommonly rough-lookin' woman, who appears to be takin' inventory, 'cause there's a circle of sod houses, and every time one of the men walks out of one he says somethin' to her, and she writes in a journal.

"You're a mule skinner?" I ask Sadie.

"Nope."

"Well, this conversation don't make no sense!"

"I *used* to be a mule skinner," she says. "Now I run this tradin' post."

I let my eyes scan the yard. "And you say Jackson Corn's dead?"

"That's right."

"Who shot him?"

"I did. Then one of my men cracked him over the head."

"Which one?"

She points to a burly, bearded man. "Jimmy."

"Jimmy cracked Corn?"

"Yup. And I don't care."

She laughs heartily.

I frown. "You're sure he's dead?"

"See that shovel?"

I nod.

"And that fresh pile of dirt behind me?"

I nod again.

"We buried him not five minutes ago."

A' course, I saw the dirt pile when I first rode up. But durin' the time we've been talkin', I come to the conclusion somethin' ain't right about it. She follows my gaze and sees the same thing I see: the dirt pile's movin'.

"Aw, shit!" she says. "Gimme a minute."

She walks over to the grave, draws her pistol, and fires six shots into the dirt.

The movement stops.

While she reloads I glance at the others and notice they ain't concerned enough to even lift their heads to see what

Sadie was shootin' at. When she walks back to where I'm sittin' she says, "This Kansas dirt's so hard you can't dig more'n two feet without breakin' your shovel."

I know all about that, and sympathize with her, since diggin' graves is one of the least things I fancy about this part of the country. Except that we ain't in Kansas, we're in Nebraska. I think about tellin' her that, but it don't seem as important as findin' out what happened to Jackson Corn and his men. So I ask her.

She says, "Jackson Corn was tradin' whiskey to the Cheyenne. I don't approve of that, and told him so."

"What did *he* say?"

"Said he didn't give a shit what I thought."

"Then what happened?"

"I punched his eye. He didn't like that, either, and told me so. Then he broke a bottle in half and came at me with it, so I drew on him and fired two shots. He wouldn't die, so Jimmy busted his skull and we buried him. But it turns out he weren't quite as dead as we thought. Now, thanks to your sharp eyes, I reckon he's finally ready to meet his maker. Which brings us to you, handsome."

"What do you mean?"

"Who are you?"

"Emmett Love, Sheriff of Dodge."

She gives me a double look, like she's heard of me. Then stares at my face, 'specially my eyes. She starts to say somethin', but changes her mind. Finally, she says, "What brings you here?"

"I came to tell Jackson Corn to stop tradin' with the Cheyenne."

"And if he refused?"

"I would've killed him."

"You're welcome," she says.

"Huh?"

"Seems I saved you a bullet."

"Eight bullets, I reckon, hard as he was to kill."

"I had 'em to spare."

I point at the men and the rough woman and say, "Your crew?"

"Yup."

"What happened to Jackson Corn's men?"

"Accordin' to him, they went to fetch a wagonload of Pine Top."

"Where do they keep it?"

"He wouldn't say. But I hope to find out when they get back."

"You plan to kill 'em?"

"Some of 'em, sure. But hopefully not all. I can use the extra help around here."

I look her over. She don't appear tough enough to ram-rod a crew and kill a group of traders as hardened as Jackson Corn's men ought to be. Then again, I've learnt to never underestimate women on the plains. Whores and trail women, especially. I consider these types of women more dangerous than gunslingers, since they can kill you a dozen ways before you know you're dyin'! And some of 'em don't look any tougher than Sadie.

Havin' said that, and havin' seen the toughest women to ever sit a saddle, I'll freely admit I ain't never seen one as hard-faced and intimidatin' as Sadie's accountant, a woman whose looks are so unfortunate, I'm thankful not to know her parents. If ever a female looked like she'd been shot at and missed, and shit at and hit, and physically able to hand-wrangle a wild longhorn, it's this one.

As for Sadie, I s'pect a woman who'd punch Jackson Corn's eye and then shoot him is the type you'd rather befriend than offend.

"I think you've got a helluva business here, Sadie."

"I agree."

"Need a partner?"

"Nope."

"Watch out for the Dog Soldiers."

"Last I heard, they were in Nebraska."

"Well, you're in Nebraska now."

"No shit?"

I point behind her.

"What now?" she says.

"Customer comin'."

CHAPTER 11

SADIE TURNS TO look, but sees nothin'.

"It's still a ways off," I say.

"What is?"

"Covered wagon."

She squints. "I see some dust bein' kicked up. Is that what you're talkin' about?"

"It's a wagon and some men."

She turns back to look at me. "What're you, an eagle?"

"Nope. Just a sheriff."

"How long before they get here?"

"An hour, maybe."

"That's more time than we need."

"For what?"

"Set a trap. It's probably Corn's men comin' back with the Pine Top. We'll kill some of 'em, and ask the others to fall in line."

Somethin' about her casualness over killin' rugged men don't feel right. "Who are you, again?"

"Sadie Nickers."

"How'd you come to covet Jackson Corn's tradin' post?"

"Black Kettle told me about it."

"*Black Kettle?* You sure about that?"

"I ought to be. I lived in his camp for six months."

"Recently?"

"No. But I spoke to him recently."

Black Kettle, a Cheyenne, was so determined to protect his people from the army, he recently signed a peace treaty with Governor Evans, of Colorado, and agreed to move his tribe to the Sand Creek Reservation. Once there, Colonel John Chivington massacred a hundred and sixty-three tribe members, mostly women and children. Black Kettle escaped, and that's the last I heard of him. If he's turned hostile, I wouldn't blame him.

"Is Black Kettle on the warpath?"

"Believe it or not, he's still pushin' for peace, though he don't trust any whites that I know of. Except me."

"Is he nearby?"

"That's none of your business."

"I got a town to protect."

"Then you better hope Black Kettle's nearby, 'cause he's the only one who can keep the Dog Soldiers at bay."

"Are *they* nearby?"

"I don't know. But that's a nasty bunch of renegades."

I scan the horizon again and ask, "You need my help?"

"For *Corn's* men?" She laughs. "Nah."

"And you'll agree not to sell whiskey to the Cheyenne?"

53

"That's why I'm here."

"Then I reckon we're good," I say.

"I reckon we are, handsome."

CHAPTER 12

WHEN I GET back to town I notice two wagons parked in front of my saloon.

Wagons I never seen before.

As I approach, Gentry runs out the front of the saloon, shoutin', "Oh, my goodness! It's Emmett Love! Hero of the Western Plains!"

I don't know what she's talkin' about, but her voice sounds strange. Before I can puzzle on it a half-dozen strangers rush out the door behind her. Three city men, dandies, run toward me, and take me by such surprise I'm compelled to draw my gun. They hit the dirt, yellin' "Don't shoot!"

Gentry yells the same thing, and adds, "They aren't *heeled*, Emmett!"

I say, "What about the women?"

"Don't be ridiculous!" she says. "Now put your gun up, crazy man. You're ruining everything!"

I have no idea what's got into Gentry, but she don't seem pleased, so I holster my gun, but keep my hand on it, just in case. One man gets to his feet and says, "You're Emmett Love?"

"I am."

A woman runs over to check on him, but looks at me and faints dead away.

I jump off Sally's back and kneel beside the woman. There's two more city women tryin' to get to the one that fainted, and when one of 'em brushes up against me, she looks me in the eye and faints as hard as the first one.

I wonder if Gentry might've tried to cook 'em somethin' to make 'em faint like that, but I know better than to ask. The men help the women to their feet, and it turns out the reason they're actin' so strange is because they're from Philadelphia.

And they've heard of me.

But what they heard, and how they heard it—is a complete and total shock.

CHAPTER 13

"YOU'RE FAMOUS, EMMETT!" Gentry says.

We're sittin' in the empty card emporium of *The Lucky Spur*. Four years ago, before the war broke out, we were so thick with cowboys and gamblers there weren't room enough to scratch your ass. Nowadays we only get card business on weekends.

And not much of it.

What surprises me, these city women are sittin' at the card table with us! Even the proper women of Old Dodge never done that. And these Philadelphia women ain't whores or sportin' women, with names like Bedpost Betty, Spoonin' Susan, or Corset Cathy. They're proper women, with names like Winifred, Amelia, and Penelope.

Gentry's keepin' a close watch on Penelope, the youngest, who's makin' doe eyes at me.

Not that the two thirty-year-olds ain't fairly swoonin' over me (they are!)

Last time proper women catered to me like this was August, 1863, when I showed up in Old Dodge after bein' held prisoner by the Union Army. Back then I was the only able-bodied man in a town of a dozen widows. A' course, them Dodge women were desperate for husbands, not infatuated, like these three, who are married to Louis, Anthony, and Oliver.

"They want to live here!" Gentry says.

"Well, that's good news," I say. "What made you choose Dodge?"

"You, sir," Oliver says.

Gentry claps her hands with delight and says, "You're famous, Emmett! You're the hero of the western plains!"

I frown.

Penelope says, "It's true, Sheriff. We've all read your astonishing exploits."

"My what?"

Oliver says, "The dime novels."

I look at Gentry.

"What's a dime novel?" I say.

The men and women look at each other, confused. Finally, Anthony says, "Amelia. Fetch the books."

Amelia heads out to the wagon and comes back a minute later carryin' three small books. She holds one up and reads, "*Emmett Love: Fastest Gun in the West.*" She puts that one beneath the other two and reads, "*Emmett Love: Man of Honor.*" She holds up the third book and reads, "*Emmett Love: Hero of the Western Plains.*"

"That's my favorite," Gentry says.

"You've read 'em?"

"No, of *course* not! Not yet, anyway. But I aim to!" She looks at Amelia and says, "If you'd be willing to part with them for an evening."

"Of course, dear," Amelia says.

She gives the books a fond look, then hands them to Gentry.

"I'll be real careful," Gentry says, and starts thumbin' through one of 'em.

While she does that, I say, "Who wrote them books? And what do they claim about me?"

Louis says, "Surely you jest! You must be aware you're the most famous man in Philadelphia!"

"I ain't never been to Philadelphia."

Gentry giggles so loud we all turn to look at her.

"What's so funny?" I say.

She reads a passage from one of the novels:

"Ladies, you will doubtless be pleased to know Emmett Love is noble of face, and possesses a chin as hard and strong as granite, eyes as clear and blue as the sapphire ring purchased by Eilley Bowers in anticipation of meeting Queen Victoria two years past, and teeth as fresh and white as the cliffs of Dover."

Penelope looks at me and sighs, which causes Gentry to give her a careful look. Not like she's angry or jealous, but not like she ain't, neither.

I say, "Who wrote them words?"

Gentry looks at the front cover and says, "Oh my goodness! I don't believe it! Burt Bagger!"

Louis says, "Your faithful chronicler."

"My what?"

"You *do* know the man," Winifred says. "Don't you? He purports to be your best friend."

"Shrug's my best friend."

They look puzzled, so I say, "I know Burt, just didn't know where he ended up. He used to own the newspaper here in town."

"And he's honest?" Winifred says. "In his writing?"

"He's been known to milk a story," I say. "And that part about Queen Victoria don't make sense. I never seen her, nor that Bowers lady, nor the cliffs of Dover, for that matter."

"Oh my," Oliver says. "I hope we haven't been hoodwinked."

"I don't know what that means," I say.

"Don't be silly, Oliver," Penelope says. "You saw how fast he drew his gun."

"Actually, I didn't. I thought it was in his hand the whole time." He pauses, then says, "You're sure he *drew* it?"

"You did, didn't you?" Penelope says.

I nod.

Louis says, "And you've killed hostile Indians?"

"A' course."

"And outlaws?"

"Well, who ain't?"

Penelope sighs so deeply if I didn't know any better, I'd swear she had eyes for me. The odd thing is her husband,

Oliver, don't seem to mind it, which causes me to wonder if sighin' among women's a common thing in Philadelphia.

She says, "Did you kill Sam Hartmann?" Under her breath she quickly adds, "Please say yes!"

I almost say somethin' rude, but remind myself these are back east folks who probably ain't got a lick a' sense. Probably don't even know it's bad luck to talk about the men you killed without spittin' first. I look around for a spot to spit, but don't want to offend the women.

"Sam Hartmann?" Penelope repeats.

"I did kill Sam," I say. "And celebrated afterward."

I jump to my feet, run to the door, and spit. Then come back in as Gentry reads:

> "Emmett Love is loyal, honest, and true; a paragon of virtue; well-known throughout Kansas, Missouri, and parts beyond as a resolute defender of women, hero to children, and protector of animals."

She smiles.

I shake my head.

Louis says, "Mr. Bagger's *Emmett Love* books are the top selling dime novels in all of Philadelphia."

I frown. "It don't make sense."

"Why not?"

"What type of man wouldn't defend women, children and animals?"

Our new neighbors look at each other and smile.

"We're home," Amelia says.

Had the day ended at that moment, things would've been perfect. But Rudy the bear suddenly came barrelin' in from the kitchen and all six Philadelphians screamed, and pissed themselves from fear.

CHAPTER 14

RUDY'S THE MOST frightened of all. It takes us ten minutes to calm him down enough to introduce him around.

Eventually everyone's comfortable with each other, and at some point Gentry and I are amazed to hear that six more families are headin' to Dodge from Philadelphia. They want to settle down in the town protected by *Emmett Love, Sheriff.*

We put the city folk up in the whores' rooms for the night, and tell the whores not to make vulgar remarks, belch, or break wind in front of 'em.

"Break wind?" Hester says. "That's some fancy-ass talk."

"How long's this bullshit gonna last?" Emma says, rubbin' her tits vigorously.

"Till we get them properly settled," Gentry says. "And don't touch yourself when talking to them."

"Lotta damn rules, if you ask me," Mary says.

63

"We didn't ask you," I say. "But listen up. Treat these people well, and more will come. After they settle into their own places, the men will come to call. But be patient. Don't flirt while their wives are here."

"What if *they* flirt with *us*?" Emma says.

"They won't," Gentry says. "So don't claim it later."

"This is our chance to build the town," I say. "Don't mess it up."

Later that night, at our house, after eatin' the biscuits and puttin' Scarlett to bed, Gentry embarrasses me by readin' some of the stories from Burt Bagger's dime novels. As she reads, I feel my face turn red, 'cause some a' the things Burt wrote about me ain't true, and them that are, ain't completely accurate. Gentry says all books are writ like that, and I should just enjoy the fact that people consider me a hero.

I study the cover and say, "Why do they call it a dime novel when the front says it costs a nickel?"

"I don't know. But the dime novels I've seen are about a hundred pages and these are only half that."

"They ought to call 'em nickel novels."

"I think it's just an expression," she says.

She studies my face a minute. "Why are you so grumpy about these books? If they help bring families to Dodge, that's a good thing."

"It ain't right for all these folks to move here on account of stories that ain't true."

"They're true in spirit, Emmett."

"Some parts ain't."

"Like what?"

"Like that Indian princess story."

"Tell me which part isn't true."

"First of all, there ain't no such thing as an Indian princess."

"That's just flowery talk, Emmett. All authors use it. It's like calling a stallion a majestic steed."

"A what?"

"My point is you might call her an Indian maid, and Burt might call her an Indian princess. It's just flowery language."

"Well, I can tell you no Indian female ever fell in love with me."

"*Why Emmett Love!*" she says, as if on the verge of bein' angry.

"What?"

"How would *you* know who's fallen in love with you?"

"Well, I reckon I'd—"

"You didn't even know *I* was in love with you till I climbed on you in a mud pond and kissed your mouth!"

As the memory comes back to me I smile. "That was the day we had the nipple contest."

"Of course you'd remember *that*," she says.

"Well, a' course! It was an important day in our lives."

"Because of the kiss," she says.

"The kiss *and* the contest. I mean, what's more important than nipples? Without nipples, tits would be pointless."

"What are you *talking* about? Wait." Her mouth curls into the smallest smile. "You made a joke just then."

"I did. Was it funny?"

"More clever than funny, I think."

"Well, it ain't easy bein' funny all the time."

"How would *you* know?"

She smiles.

I stare at her blankly till she says, "I was making a little joke myself just then."

"Oh."

I try to force a chuckle, but she can tell I didn't get her joke. I say, "If I was the judge, you'd win the nipple contest every time."

She thinks about that a minute, then frowns.

"Now what's wrong?"

"I lost that nipple contest on the White River when you voted against me."

"I didn't vote against you, Gentry. I didn't vote at *all!*"

"That's what I'm talking about. You gave me no support."

"It wouldn't have been fair for me to vote."

"Why not?"

"'Cause I'd already developed feelin's for you. On account of the kiss."

She stares at my face, then hers breaks out into one a' them legendary Gentry smiles.

"What?"

"Don't tell me you're not honest, noble, and true, Emmett Love."

"Why not?"

"Because you're the most honest man who ever lived. You didn't even vote for me when doing so would've helped you get in my pants!"

"I s'pect I could easily become the world's most dishonest man if it meant gettin' in your pants."

She smiles.

I say, "But if you believe I'm honest you'll know why I can't let them people think I saved some Indian princess who fell in love with me and talked the chief into sparin' the town."

"Oh, Emmett," she sighs.

"What?"

"It's just true stories mixed together to sound more romantic. You *did* save an Indian maid once. You told me so."

"And Burt knows the story, too," I say. "But he knew she was a squaw, not a princess. And I saved her from bein' raped, not killed. By white men, not Indians. And I didn't kill eight Indians in that tribe, like Burt claims."

"You killed all four Indian scouts when they were heading away from their camps in different directions, did you not?"

"Yes, but not the same night I saved the squaw."

"And how do you know those men wouldn't have killed her if you hadn't killed them first?"

"Well..."

"And have you killed eight warriors from the same tribe during a battle?"

"Well, a' course I have. But that ain't the point."

She shakes her head and clucks. "Emmett, you need to accept the fact you're a hero. Now be quiet about it, and get over yourself."

And that was that.

67

The next day, while givin' the new folks a tour of the construction site for the school house and church, Penelope says Burt's written not three, but ten *Emmett Love* dime novels!

I sure hope I don't end up the laughin' stock of Dodge.

CHAPTER 15

THE FOLKS FROM Philadelphia are disappointed to learn we only got a handful of businesses, and an unfinished church and schoolhouse.

Their faces drop further when I tell 'em there ain't but thirty full-time residents in New Dodge, includin' parlor ladies and children.

"I know it's a poor start, but we're four years into the war, and Kansas has been hit hard. More than 18,000 men have already been killed, and them that survive won't have farms or ranches to come home to."

"Why not?" Amelia says.

"When soldiers come across a farm or ranch they take all they can carry and burn down the rest. So I've been puttin' most of my hopes on the folks travelin' the Westward and Santa Fe trails, figurin' they'd stop here for supplies and maybe a drink or two, and then I'd talk the nicer ones into settlin' down with us."

"Clearly that's not working," Amelia says.

"That's 'cause most of 'em have their hearts set on Colorado. I swear, if I have to hear from one more traveler how sweet the air is in Colorado, and how beautiful the mountains, I'm liable not to be responsible for my actions!"

"There *is* a case to be made for beautiful scenery," Amelia says.

I frown. "In my opinion communities are built by folks who'd rather look at crops than mountaintops."

Winifred says, "I'm still concerned about the church and schoolhouse. In *Emmett Love Saves Dodge City*, Burt Bagger speaks of a fine church and schoolhouse."

I explain how I moved the town twelve miles north so we could take advantage of the trade from the Westward and Santa Fe trails. Then say, "Old Dodge had thirty businesses, a church and schoolhouse. They're still usable, if you don't mind travelin' twelve miles."

"Is it dangerous?" Winifred asks.

"There's less protection there, but it ain't deserted. Half the townspeople still live there."

"Well *that's* good news! But why haven't they moved?"

"They're waitin' till the new houses and businesses get built."

"In that case, we should be building houses and businesses."

"We should, indeed."

"Then why aren't you?"

"Well..."

Winifred frowns. "Sounds like you need a mayor."

"We've got a fine mayor. But she still lives in Old Dodge."

"*She?*" Penelope says.

"Yes, ma'am."

"A woman *mayor?*" Amelia says. "Are you *serious?*"

"I am."

"What's her name?"

"Margaret Stallings."

"Can we meet her?"

"A' course. I already sent notice to May Gray, in Old Dodge. I s'pect she'll want to host a welcome party for you."

"Why haven't she and Margaret moved here?"

"They're partial to their houses. They've got spots picked out, but don't plan to move till the town grows bigger."

"What's the hold up on construction?"

"We ain't got enough workers to finish the new houses, let alone the new church and schoolhouse."

"Who built the saloon and sheriff's office?" Louis asks.

"And the stable?" Amelia adds. "And your beautiful home?"

"Well..."

"I've noted the construction," Louis says. "It's quality work."

I hesitate to tell 'em the true story of what happened to the workers, but I reckon it's somethin' that needs to be said. I take a deep breath and ask, "What's your opinion of our parlor ladies?"

The women look at each other, then at their husbands. The husbands look uneasy. Finally Winifred says, "We spent half the night talking about it. To be honest, we don't approve of establishments that serve alcohol, encourage gambling, or employ soiled doves."

"Ma'am?"

"Soiled doves."

I shake my head. "You mean prairie doves?"

"Is that what you call them?"

"Well, we get more prairie dogs out here than doves."

She frowns. "I'm speaking of ladies of ill repute."

I stare at her.

She says, "I'll not say the word." She looks at her husband for help.

Louis leans into my ear and whispers, "*Prostitutes.*"

"Oh."

"Nevertheless," Winifred continues, "we're fully aware we're the outsiders in this equation, and our values were formed in a different society, under different circumstances. It wouldn't be fair for us to impose our beliefs on others the moment we arrive in a new place. It would be as if you and Gentry moved to an Indian village and didn't approve of their customs."

It bothers me hearin' her words, because the Indian way of life is disappearin' fast, and I don't want my saloon or whorehouse to suffer a similar fate. While western towns need proper women, they also need whiskey, whores, and gamblin'. And of the three, they need whores the most.

Gentry calls it a delicate balance, meanin' there's two groups in every town that are natural enemies of the other:

moral and immoral. But both sides need each other. If we didn't have whiskey, cards and whores, the preacher wouldn't have nothin' to preach about, the proper women wouldn't have nothin' to rail against, and kids wouldn't have bad examples to help 'em learn virtue. On the other hand, gamblin' gives men hope, liquor gives 'em a way to forget their troubles, and whores help keep marriages together because proper women are often too tired or cranky to pleasure their men in an enthusiastic manner after puttin' in a full day's work. Gentry says a good whore can keep a bad man from beatin' his wife and kids.

What proper women don't seem to understand is whores are the backbone of a western town's economy. They bring outside money into the community. Cowboys and miners get paid on Friday afternoon, and want to enjoy themselves. They'll drink, whore, and gamble. Or drink and whore. Or just whore. What they won't do is buy a big meal in a fancy restaurant, or spend the night in a hotel. They sleep for free at the livery with their horses, or on the plains far enough out of town so as not to disturb the residents. If they eat, it'll be in the saloon where they're drinkin'. They might spend a small sum on boots or saddle repair and the like, but they put very little cash into the town's moral businesses.

They put their money where they put their peckers.

That's good for the town because whores spend their money enthusiastically at the general store, dry goods store, milliner's, dressmakers, leatherworks, and other moral-type establishments. Whores attract money from outside sources and move it into the local economy, which benefits every man, woman, and child in the community.

This delicate balance is why the whores tolerate the proper women and church-goers that publicly shun 'em, and it's why we set rules that allow whores to shop in respectable stores two hours a day, Monday through Saturday. It's why they're allowed to eat at the fancy restaurants on Tuesday and Thursday nights (not that we've got any fancy restaurants in Dodge at the moment).

It's a delicate balance.

You get the feelin' the proper women are always on the edge of railin' against the whores, drinkin', and gamblin', 'cause them things attract their husbands and sons same as they attract cowboys, miners, fur traders, and buffalo hunters.

Dodge will be a wonderful place to live as long as the preacher and mayor understand why both types of businesses are important to the town. Though he ain't currently got a church, Reverend Murphy understands it, and though she ain't got much of a town to manage, Margaret Stallings is also on board. I think these Philadelphia women will like Margaret, till they learn she tolerates gamblin', drinkin', and whorin'.

Amelia says, "I'm delighted to hear you've elected a woman to the post. I commend your foresight. Such enlightened progressivism is unheard of in Philadelphia."

I know what *delighted* means, and figure all her other words add up to a compliment, so I say, "Thank you."

She says, "What do the...ah...women in your saloon have to do with the slowdown in housing construction?"

"Well…"

Winifred says, "Wait. We need to come to an agreement on a title of reference for these women who peddle their flesh in your saloon. Might we use the term we're familiar with, soiled doves?"

Before answerin', I think about how feisty our whores can be around proper women. A few years ago half the town discovered Katherine Plenty had three large freckles on her bosom when Constance attacked her over an unfortunate remark. Had we waited ten seconds longer to intervene, Mrs. Plenty would have been completely naked, and stabbed to death.

"They might let you call 'em doves," I say. "But I'd recommend against the 'soiled' part."

Winifred frowns.

"What do they call themselves?"

I bite my lip, then motion to Louis. When he comes close, I whisper it.

His face turns ash gray. He stands there dumbstruck, with his head cocked, as if to hear my next whisper, but since I only had the one word to say, I take a few steps back. Finally he turns to the others and says, "There is still work to be done on this matter, but for now I suggest we simply refer to them as parlor ladies."

Winifred stares at her husband a moment. "Very well, Louis. So tell me, Mr. Love, what did your…parlor ladies…have to do with this construction delay?"

I tell 'em how Gentry came into a great inheritance a few months back, which gave us the means to hire twenty men from Saint Jo to help us haul wood and materials from Old Dodge to the current location.

"They stayed long enough to help me build my saloon and sheriff's office, but when the wagons arrived from Saint Jo with the iron bars for my jail, some of the Saint Jo wives followed in their own wagon to surprise their husbands. Unfortunately, they found some of their menfolk in the saloon, spendin' their hard-earned money on whiskey and...parlor women. The wives were so upset they dragged every last man back to Saint Jo the next mornin', and we ain't seen 'em since."

"I see."

"I've got the money to spend, but no workers to spend it on."

"The solution is simple," she says.

"It is?"

"Of course. We'll simply travel to Saint Jo, meet the wives, and assure them their men will not step foot in the saloon."

"How do you aim to keep twenty men from enterin' the saloon at night?"

She says, "Amelia? Please enlighten Mr. Love about the mistake he made with regard to the construction crew."

Amelia says, "You paid the wrong people."

"What do you mean?"

"You should have paid the wives, not the husbands. And in advance. From now on we'll take the money to the wives every month, in advance, until the job is done. In the meantime, you'll provide meals and necessities, but refuse them credit. Without cash or credit, they won't be able to buy drinks, participate in sporting games, or proposition parlor ladies."

Noting the look on my face, Winifred says, "Don't look so stunned, Sheriff. It's simple economics."

I shake my head and grin like a brain-fevered fox. "Them simple economics is about the smartest thing I ever heard."

"Simply tell us where to go and to whom we should speak," Winifred says.

"I reckon I should go with you."

"You? Pardon me for saying so, but you're the *last* person they'd trust."

"And anyway," Amelia says, "You'll be too busy to go."

"Why's that?"

Penelope says, "Why, you'll be in Philadelphia, of course!"

"Philadelphia?"

"Of course! You said you wanted to build a town, did you not? How better to do so than by enticing Philadelphians to move here, instead of the Rockies? What you said about communities being built by those who prefer crops to mountaintops is more than poetic, it's practical. There are hundreds of families in Philly looking for an excuse to come west. They need only the smallest nudge. We six will write letters about what we've seen, and explain our plans for the future, and you'll deliver them to the proper people in Philadelphia."

"Me?"

"Of course! *Everyone* knows the name Emmett Love! You and Gentry will take the city by storm! Between us and our friends who'll be arriving soon, we'll have the money and manpower to build our own homes. We'll choose our building lots before you leave. If you're serious about funding the business construction, this town will be thriving within the year."

"You want Gentry and me to travel to Philadelphia?"

"Why wouldn't you? The war will be over any day now."

"You think?"

"It's a certainty."

"Which side's gonna win?"

Penelope looks at me like I'm loony. Like the answer's so obvious I shouldn't have asked the question. I ain't worried about it. I figure when the war ends it'll make enough news that someone will say who won.

CHAPTER 16

THE DAY I met her, Gentry told me there were five things she always wanted to do.

One, ride on a stagecoach.

I told her a hundred times she's gonna hate stagecoach ridin'. It's noisy, bumpy, and the seats are hard as rocks.

"It's not the ride I'm after," she says. "It's the experience."

It'll be a short experience, I reckon.

Two, ride on a steamboat.

I never tried to discourage her from steamboats, since I always wanted to ride one myself.

Three, see a stage show.

I've seen a few shows in my day, and learned the good ones are great and the bad ones are terrible. I aim to make sure Gentry's first one is a grand experience.

Four, use a water closet.

A water closet is a sort of indoor outhouse, where you do your business while sittin' on what they call a toilet, which is a large bowl with a seat above it. The bottom of the bowl has a pipe connected to it. There's a pull chain attached to a box full of water above this contraption, and when you finish your business on the toilet, you pull the chain and whatever you put inside the bowl suddenly disappears down a pipe and goes outside the house into a ditch. If this is a true thing that really works, I s'pect it'll catch on with womenfolk, 'cause there ain't a more dangerous place for women and girls at night than an outhouse. Most rapes by strangers occur when a woman or girl is headin' to or from an outhouse after dark.

Gentry heard about water closets from the same person who hired tutors to teach her to read, write, and speak proper English: her former husband, David Wilkins. Wilkins turned out to be a horrible husband, but he was worldly, and when he weren't beatin' or threatenin' Gentry, he told her about things like Christmas trees and water closets. He said he saw them things in London, England, ten years ago. Said all the rich people had Christmas trees, and that he saw not one, but *ten* water closets in an all-glass buildin' called *The Crystal Palace*, that was built for the Great Exhibition of 1851.

The fifth thing Gentry always wanted to do is so fanciful I won't be a party to it, but it's my fault it wound up on her list. The very first day I met her at Shingles Dance Hall in Rolla, Missouri I told her about Lola Montez, the richest and most famous whore west of the Mississippi. I told Gentry that Lola took a champagne bath every day and wiped her ass with rose petals. Gentry's eyes went big as saucers, and that's how takin' a champagne bath got on her wish list. I suppose it's good to have somethin' to dream about, but where on earth would a man find enough champagne in the same town to fill a bathtub? And what would somethin' like that cost?

I never thought much about makin' her dreams come true, 'cause, like I say, they seemed so fanciful. But these Philadelphians are makin' me wonder if this trip idea might be a chance for Gentry to do some a' them things.

Not the champagne bath, of course, but maybe...

"Do they have water closets in Philadelphia?" I ask.

"Sadly, no," Penelope says. "But we've all heard about them."

Okay, so no indoor outhouse and no champagne bath for Gentry. But I can certainly take her on a stagecoach ride. And I'm sure there's...

"Is there a theater there? One that has good stage shows?"

"There are many. But the best is the Walnut Street Theater. It has air conditioning."

"What's that?"

"When it's hot outside, the inside of the theater is cool."

"You're joshin' me!"

"No. I've been there. We all have. Is there anything else you'd like to see or do on your trip?"

"Me and Gentry always wanted to ride a steamboat."

Anthony says, "For a real steamboat experience, I recommend you board at Cincinnati. You can journey all the way to Pittsburgh."

"Is it a long ride?"

"Days. But you'll be quite comfortable, believe me. These are genuine sternwheelers. They're massive, with huge ceilings and grand ballrooms."

"Have you ever ridden a really big one?" I ask Penelope.

She blushes and looks around. "Sir?"

"I thought maybe you'd tell Gentry about the experience. Includin' what to wear, and what to expect, and so forth."

"Oh," she says. "Well, of course, I'd be delighted, Mr. Love."

"I'm hopin' to make her more excited about the trip than nervous."

"Is she nervous?"

"More so about leavin' Scarlett, I think."

"Speaking of Scarlett," Amelia says.

"Yes?"

The women look at each other. Then Amelia says, "We couldn't help but notice when she's nearby..."

"Yes?"

Her husband, Anthony, says, "The child seems to have a special quality. We feel better when we're around her."

"That's quite a compliment," I say. "Most folks think Scarlett's natural disposition leans toward gloomy. Can't blame her for that, she's been through a lot. But Gentry's struggled mighty hard to make her cheerful."

Penelope looks frustrated. "We're not speaking so much about her disposition as her..." "Her what"

I study her face. She's tryin' to say somethin', but tryin' *not* to at the same time. She gives it another go. "When we first arrived we were tired from the long wagon journey. We were swollen, bruised, and sore. When Scarlett entered the room, we suddenly felt better. When she left, the aches and pains returned immediately. When she came back in, we felt better again."

"More like euphoric," Amelia adds.

"We didn't attribute it to Scarlett till later," Winifred says.

I frown.

It's started.

CHAPTER 17

AFTER LEAVIN' THE Philadelphia folks I climb onto the Lucky Spur's roof and whistle my wood warbler.

A minute later Shrug joins me, and I tell him about the new people, and how they plan to re-hire the builders from Saint Jo. I tell him they think Gentry and me should go to Philadelphia to lecture about the virtues of movin' to Dodge City instead of Colorado or California.

Gentry and Scarlett swear Shrug can talk. And accordin' to Shrug's former lover, Phoebe Thayer, he speaks not only English, but is fluent in French and has a "gorgeous" singin' voice.

I don't know if he can talk or not, but he don't talk to me.

Gentry thinks it's 'cause I never asked him if he could talk durin' the two years we traveled together. I say, "Who'd have to ask someone if they can *talk*? Wouldn't the person just talk if he could?"

I think the reason he don't talk to me is 'cause he likes bein' around someone who doesn't *need* him to. Or maybe he can't talk at all and them who say he can have been joshin' me all along. I could always ask him, but I figure if he wants to talk, he'll talk. If he don't, he won't.

We're sittin' on a tin roof, and it's late March, which means there's enough sun to make it warmer than what I consider comfortable, but Shrug don't seem to notice. He's havin' fun pretendin' he's bowin' down to me, and it suddenly dawns on me what he's referrin' to.

"You heard about the dime novels?"

He nods.

"I don't know if you can read," I say, "but if so, don't read 'em. They're horseshit."

He holds up two fingers.

"You read *two*? Where'd you get 'em?"

He grins, but don't sign.

I say, "How long have you known about these books?"

He signs out a year.

"*What? A year?*"

He laughs.

"Why didn't you say somethin' before now?"

He signs I never asked him.

I roll my eyes, then tell him how Rose has been gettin' into Scarlett's head, teachin' her stuff, and how Gentry's upset about it. He signs it's a good thing. I agree. Then tell I him how Scarlett told Gentry she needed to go to the river to fetch some snake shit.

85

Shrug falls down laughin'. When he mimes pickin' up tiny pieces of snake shit, I nearly fall down laughin', too.

After a few minutes I ask, "Have you heard from Rose?"

Shrug nods.

"You have any idea when she's comin'?"

He looks puzzled.

I say, "You don't mean she's already here."

He nods.

"Where?"

He signs she's at my house.

"Now?"

He nods.

"Why the hell didn't you *say* so?"

He signs I didn't ask.

I head to the edge of the roof. Before climbing off, I say, "If I go to Philadelphia, will you watch over the town?"

He nods.

CHAPTER 18

WHEN I APPROACH my house I see Rose's buckboard. But when I whistle my wood warbler, only Gentry comes out to greet me.

"Where's Rose?

"She took Scarlett."

"What do you mean, 'took her?'"

"She lectured me, then took Scarlett for a walk."

"Lectured you how?"

"She told me Scarlett was just starting to bloom. Then she chastised me for correcting Scarlett's language."

"The snake shit thing?"

Gentry nods.

"What did she say about it?"

"She asked if I ever cut open a snake's head and studied its brain."

"Have you?"

"Of course not, Emmett!"

"Then what was she talkin' about?"

"She said I need to be more understanding about how Scarlett phrases things because snakes are simple creatures with very limited brain power. She says it's hard enough to convey the word *shit* to a snake, and if Scarlett tries to come up with an alternative word, there's no telling how the snake might react. Why are you looking at me like that?"

"Because I can't believe we're having this conversation."

"Well, you'd best believe it, because she's taken our daughter for a talk. Then they're going to the river."

"To fetch snake shit?"

Gentry presses her lips tightly together. "Yes, Emmett, to fetch snake shit."

She sighs. "I've tried to teach her a better way of talking than you and I grew up with, but now, thanks to your friend, it appears our daughter converses with snakes. I knew there'd be adjustments to make after giving birth, and I knew there was only so much I'd be able to teach Scarlett, and that eventually I'd have to turn the task of furthering her education over to someone else. But really, Emmett? *Rose?* I suppose from now on the word *shit* will be tossed about in our home with the same frequency as *hello* and *nice to meet you.*" She looks at me and adds, "I wonder if that pleases you?"

"Well, if the things Rose is teachin' Scarlett leads to savin' the town I'd be happy to say *shit* day and night, wouldn't you?"

"That's not the point."

"What's the point?"

"We're allowing witches to educate our child, and rep-
tiles to influence her speech."

"Just one."

"What?"

"It's just the one witch."

"So far."

"What did she say about Scarlett startin' to bloom? I
hope she don't mean the same type of bloomin' Enorma did
this year."

Gentry frowns. "She's three, Emmett, not fourteen."
She shakes her head. "Rose said the same thing Wayne told
us. That someday people would start following Scarlett
around, and camp in our yard because being near her takes
away their pain and makes them feel better."

"The Philadelphia folks noticed it."

"I've noticed it, too. Look."

She lifts her dress to mid-thigh. A couple days ago she
was kicked by Clara's cow. Yesterday mornin' she had a terrible bruise. Today it's gone.

"That the same leg?" I say.

"Of course, Emmett."

"You're sure?"

"Positive."

"Let me see the other one."

She lifts her dress so I can compare both thighs.

"Maybe it was a little higher up," I say.

She starts to lift her skirt higher to prove I'm wrong, but
realizes at the last second I'm flirtin' with her.

"Nice try," she says, but her voice ain't as playful as usual. She lets her dress fall back in place, which means I can't even see her shoes now.

I ask, "Did Rose say where they were goin', or how long they'd be?"

"She said they were taking a stroll through town. Where were you, that you didn't see them?"

"On the roof of the Spur."

"Why?"

"I was visitin' with Shrug. He's the one told me Rose was in town."

"And you invited him to dinner, of course."

"Uh..."

She shakes her head. "Emmett? Seriously? Wayne's your best friend."

"I'm embarrassed to say it never crossed my mind."

"Give him a call."

I go out to the front yard and make my whistle.

CHAPTER 19

SCARLETT SAYS, "THAT'S Papa's whistle. Should I answer?"

"You tell me."

Scarlett closes her eyes, cocks her head to listen, then says, "Chipping sparrow."

"Which means?"

"He's talking to Shrug."

They resume their walk. As they approach the sheriff's office, Rose points to the dry goods store and says, "There!"

"Ma'am?"

"That's where you'll see him for the first time."

"Who?"

"Jed Coulter."

"Who's that?"

"Your true love. Want a peek?"

Scarlett nods.

Rose touches her shoulder and says, "See the girl coming out of the sheriff's office?"

Scarlett squints. "Yes, ma'am."

"She's fourteen years old. Beautiful, don't you think?"

"Yes, ma'am."

"See her staring across the street? She's looking at a young man, loading a wagon. Do you see him?"

"Yes, ma'am."

"Good. Now watch how he pauses. He *feels* something powerful. Study his expression when he looks up. Wait for it. *There!* See that look?"

"Yes, ma'am."

"That's it. That's what love looks like."

"He loves her?"

"He does."

"Does she love him?"

"Yes."

"Is that me?"

Rose beams. "You have a fine mind, Scarlett. That's why I chose you. That, and because we're related."

"We are?"

Rose says, "Yes. On your mother's side. What I don't understand is why I'm babbling on so much. Guess I'm starved for conversation."

"Does Jed have a fine mind?"

Rose laughs. "*Jed?* Oh, God, no! He'd be smarter with sawdust between his ears. But that's okay, I chose him for a different reason. Now pay attention. Do you see him standing there, at the wagon?"

"No, ma'am."

"Use your mind to see him."

"I see him."

"Good. Eleven years from now, when he spies you coming out of the sheriff's office, he'll look up, you'll stare straight into his eyes without turning away."

Rose leans down, gives her a hug. "This is how you'll feel."

Scarlett gasps.

Rose ends the hug and says, "You'll fall in love the moment your eyes meet, and he'll fall in love even deeper than you."

"Are Jed and me going to get married?"

Rose smiles. "Of course. And I'll deliver your baby the following year. Any questions?"

"Will I be happy?"

A look of surprise crosses Rose's face. "What an odd question!"

"Will I?" Scarlett repeats.

Rose pauses a moment, then says, "Some of the time."

Rose stands, closes her eyes, and says, "He's a wicked man. Worst I've known in a century. If ever a man needed killing, it's him."

"Jed?"

"Jed's father, Bose Rennick. But don't worry, Bose knows nothing about Jed."

"Will our baby be nice?"

Rose frowns. "I sure hope so. You'd think after all this time I'd have a better handle on selective breeding. But there are no guarantees. Nothing else I've tried has worked, so I went all in with this one. It's desperation, nothing more."

"Ma'am?"

"I figured, why not match the best with the worst? I mean, how bad could it be, right?" She pauses, then adds, "Embarrassing to admit all this." She looks at her young apprentice and says, "It's not important."

She touches Scarlett's forehead and says, "You don't remember any of this. It's all forgotten. Sometimes it just helps me to think out loud. Let's move on to our lessons."

Scarlett blinks. "Lessons?"

"Animal coming."

"Ma'am?"

"Pay attention! Animal coming! What is it?"

"I don't know."

"Concentrate! Danger!"

Scarlett concentrates.

"Nothing?" Rose says.

"No, ma'am."

"It's practically on *top* of us! Try harder!"

Scarlett shrugs.

Rose points to the open field across from the sheriff's office and says, "This isn't good. We need to work on this."

Scarlett suddenly sees the feral dog racing through the high grass, coming toward them.

She screams.

"Don't show fear!" Rose says.

The wild dog slows as it approaches them. When he's ten feet away, Scarlett slowly positions her body behind Rose. The dog pauses, sniffs the air. Makes a low, guttural sound. The hair on his neck and shoulders stands straight up. He takes two steps forward.

Scarlett grips Rose's hand tightly.

"Shh," Rose says. "Be still. Be brave."

The cur lowers his body, ready to leap. He takes a slow step forward, then snarls, bares his teeth, lets loose a deep, rumbling growl.

Scarlett screams again.

The dog tries to circle Rose.

"He wants your throat," she says.

The dog suddenly leaps in the air toward Scarlett's throat.

Scarlett lets out a deafening scream, and the dog explodes in midair.

She continues screaming, and it's all Rose can do to calm her down. By then, Shrug's kneeling over what's left of the carcass. He grins at Rose and tosses the largest hunk over his shoulder before bounding off into the open field.

"Guess he won't be having dinner with us," Rose says.

They both hear something at the same time and turn their heads to see an out-of-shape man running toward them from the far end of town. They wait for him to close the distance, watch him slow to a stop a dozen feet away. He puts his hands on his knees and gasps for breath. Panting loudly, he says, "Release the child."

"Mind your own business," Rose says.

"I'm Jim Bigsby. I own the livery stable."

"That must make you the proudest man in town. Now back away before I get annoyed."

"Ever heard of Emmett Love?" He points to Scarlett. "That's his daughter. You don't want to cross *him*, I'll wager."

"Go back to your horses, Jim."

Jim's hand slowly edges toward his holster.

Rose says, "If you're Emmett's friend you should know Scarlett's middle name."

"I do, indeed."

"Then ponder this: she's named after me."

It takes a few seconds to sink in. When it does, Jim says, "You're *Rose*? The one who—"

Rose shows him an icy smile. "The one who *what*, Jim?"

Jim is suddenly quite uncomfortable. He wants to haul ass, but doesn't want to leave Scarlett in danger.

"Scarlett?" he says. "I heard screaming. Are you okay?"

"She's fine," Rose says. "See her holding my hand?"

"What *happened* here?"

"I'm teaching her survival skills. Go play with your horses."

"Scarlett?"

Scarlett composes herself, then says, "I'm all right, Mr. Bigsby. Sorry if I worried you."

Jim does a double take. "You sound like a twelve-year-old."

"I got smarter."

"You sure did. But when?"

"Just now."

"You're sure you're all right?"

"Yes, sir." She pauses. "Mr. Bigsby?"

"Yes, honey?"

"Sorry about your wife."

"My *wife*? Clara? What about her?"

Scarlett feels the sudden pressure of Rose's hand on her shoulder.

Jim repeats, "What's this about Clara?"

Scarlett says, "I mean I'm sorry she has to feed all those folks every night."

Jim says, "Well, that's what neighbors do when there's not food enough to go around." He looks at her again and says, "I can't believe the difference in you since the last time I saw you."

"Please tell Miss Clara I said hello."

Jim nods, and starts walking away. When he gets to the corner, he turns and gives them one last, long look before heading back to the livery.

Rose looks at the wild dog remnants covering Scarlett's hair, face, and clothes.

"I don't understand how he got so close without you knowing. Or why you couldn't control your fear."

"I'm sorry."

"On the other hand, I've never seen anyone blow up an animal by screaming. So there's that."

Scarlett says, "Why didn't *you* stop him?"

"I'm the one who sent for him."

"Why?"

"To see how close he'd come before you sniffed him out. When you couldn't, I decided to let him bite you."

Scarlett's eyes go wide. "*What?*"

"I thought if you got bit it might help you learn to sniff out wild dogs in the future."

"You were going to let him *bite* me?"

"Just once. For the lesson, though I wouldn't have let it hurt too much. But you handled it fine, except for the mess. You *should* have known the dog was coming. You also should have known about the rattlesnake in the alley by the sheriff's office. Then, you could have—"

"I *did* know about the snake. It's still there."

Rose looks at her. "Why didn't you make it shake its rattle? That would have scared the dog."

"I couldn't."

Rose frowns. "Why not? It's a simple command."

"I didn't want Percy to get hurt."

"Percy?"

She points to the vacant street. After a moment, two girls and a small boy turn the corner and come into view a block away. They're playing tag.

Scarlett says, "In my head, the dog ran from the snake and killed Percy."

Rose looks confused. "You saw that happen in your mind?"

"Yes, ma'am."

"You can tell the future?"

"I don't know."

Rose says, "But you didn't see the dog coming."

"No, ma'am."

"I wonder why." She thinks on it a minute, then says, "Do you have any ideas about it?"

Scarlett shrugs. "I don't have lots of ideas. I'm only three."

"Good point, but—"

"And you've only taught me whistles and snakes."

"True."

As they head back home, Rose says, "What was that business about Jim's wife?"

"She's sick. She'll be dead soon."

"How do you know?"

Scarlett shrugs.

They walk quietly till Rose says, "That's an amazing scream you've got."

"Thank you."

"Is this the first time you used it?"

"No, ma'am."

"But it's the first time you've killed?"

"By screaming?"

Rose gives her a look. "Do you know other ways to kill?"

"Yes, ma'am."

"How many?"

"Lots."

"And *have* you killed?"

Scarlett pauses.

Rose says, "It'll be our little secret."

Scarlett motions for Rose to lean over, and whispers in her ear for a long time. The more she says, the wider Rose's eyes grow. When Scarlett finishes her confession, Rose says, "Don't repeat this to anyone else for as long as you live. Understand?"

"Yes, ma'am."

"You can tell *me* these sorts of things, but no one else, okay?"

Scarlett nods.

"Before we get to your house is there anything you want to ask me about?"

"Yes, ma'am."

"Go ahead."

"Am I different from everyone else?"

"Yes. I mean, we all have special gifts, but most people don't know how to use them. But yours are stronger and more valuable than most. And more dangerous."

"Will we always be friends?"

"Will you promise to keep your baby alive till she marries?"

"Yes, ma'am."

"Then yes, we'll always be friends."

They walk a few more steps, and Rose says, "Why did you ask me that?"

"Because I remember everything you said. Even after you touched my head."

"Thanks for telling me that. Your gifts are powerful, but very confusing. I can't believe you're not going to live a full century." She stops, puts both hands on Scarlett's ears, closes her eyes, concentrates.

Then smiles. "*That* ought to do it. Now, tell me what I just said."

"You said my gifts are powerful, but very confusing. You can't believe I'm not going to live a full centry."

"Shit!"

"Don't say shit in front of Mama."

"Okay."

CHAPTER 20

WHEN GENTRY SEES Rose and Scarlett walking through the front gate, covered in blood, fur, and what looks like animal guts, she screams and runs out the door, with me close behind.

Rose puts her hand up. "Don't be alarmed, she's not hurt. It looks worse than it is."

I'm thinkin' that's good to hear, 'cause it looks pretty damn bad. So bad that after Gentry calms down she says, "It'd be easier to have another child than to clean this one up."

Rose says, "I'll take care of it."

"What happened?" I say.

Rose starts to say somethin', then changes her mind. "What does it look like?"

"Like nothin' I ever saw."

"Try to imagine something."

"Well, if a wolf swallowed a burnin' stick a' dynamite, and blew up in Scarlett's arms she'd be a bit cleaner..."

"Go with that," Rose says. "It's a better story."

Gentry says, "I know you're teaching her things. But I can't allow any activity that puts her life in danger."

"I understand," Rose says.

Gentry looks at Scarlett, then Rose. "What really happened here?"

Rose laughs. "I know this looks bad, but it's really nothing more than...how would you describe these stains, Scarlett?"

Our daughter looks at us with wide, innocent eyes and says, "Animal fur, nuts, and berries."

I pull some pieces of bone and cartilage from her hair and hold it up.

Rose says, "We may have gotten a little carried away in our teaching game."

The two of them look thick as thieves.

"This mess is the result of a *game*?" I say.

"A teaching game," Scarlett says. "About wild life, and animal innards and... I had the best time *ever!*"

Gentry takes a deep breath and says, "Rose, I know this teaching is for a good cause, and we're grateful you chose Scarlett...I think. But if possible, I'd ask you to be less exuberant in your games from now on. Scarlett has a limited amount of clothing."

"I'll be more careful," Rose says. "But don't worry about her clothes. They'll be good as new by morning. As will mine."

Gentry looks at Scarlett's dress and says, "That won't happen."

Rose smiles. "Trust me."

Gentry gives me a look.

I turn and head back inside to clean my guns and wait for dinner.

Speakin' of which, Rose brought some canned meats and vegetables with her, to spare Gentry the work of tryin' to cook. After enjoyin' a bigger meal than I expected, I walk Rose a short ways from the house and say, "I want to thank you for what you did."

"When?"

"David Wilkins? Gentry's husband?"

"What about him?"

"You froze time so Gentry could kill him. You opened the cage I was in so I could save Scarlett. You saved our lives."

Rose says, "Can I be honest?"

"A' course."

"I didn't do those things."

"A' *course* you did! Shrug said he went all the way to Bowie Country to ask for your help."

"That's true, but I told him no."

"But then you changed your mind."

She shakes her head.

"Then how do you explain—"

"I'll say this only once: don't let anyone terrify Scarlett. Or make her furious."

"What?"

"Ever."

CHAPTER 21

NEXT MORNIN' I wake up to the smell of bacon in the fryin' pan.

I enter the room and exchange good mornin's with everyone. Scarlett's sittin' at the table, sketchin' on one of the many pieces of paper Rose brought as a gift.

"Look, Papa!" she says.

I walk over to see what she's drawin'. Whatever it is, I can't make it out.

"Show me when it's finished," I say.

"Okay."

"I never seen so many pages of paper in all my life! That was right nice of you, Rose."

"I thought it would be good for Scarlett to express her visions on paper," she says, taking a sip of Gentry's coffee.

"Sorry about the coffee," Gentry says. "I know it's awful."

Rose says, "Did you forget to boil the water?"

I try not to smile.

Gentry says, "I can't seem to get the water hot enough to boil."

"How often are you fueling your stove?"

"Every day."

"Problem solved. You need to refuel it every hour."

"Seriously?"

"And you need to empty the trays every night to give your fires proper airflow."

Gentry says, "I'm better at baking."

"Really? Good for you!" Rose says. "Baking's a hard-learned skill."

"Well, truth be told, biscuits are all I know," Gentry confesses. She fetches the batch she made yesterday and places them on the table. As I reach for one, she slaps my hand, playfully.

"We have a guest," she says.

Rose says, "Biscuits have simple ingredients, but they're hard to perfect." She picks one up, takes a bite, and smiles.

"Why, these are *excellent*, Gentry!"

I can see Gentry's pleased to hear that, since Rose is the best cook we know.

Gentry says, "You're being kind. I *do* try, but I got a late start in the kitchen."

Rose says, "I'd be honored to help you."

"I expect it'll take magic."

Rose raises an eyebrow.

Gentry says, "Oh. I didn't mean to imply—"

Rose waves her off. "It's timing, not magic. Knowing which foods need which fires, and when and how to adjust the wood."

"Can you teach me how to bake pies and cakes?"

"If I were you, I'd start with stews."

My ears perk up at that.

"Stews?" Gentry says.

"Much more practical. And unlike baking, a good stew requires less tending, once you get your fire right."

"What kind of stew can you teach me to make?"

I jump into the conversation. "Rabbit. Squirrel. Deer. Duck. Chicken. Pig. You name it, I'll eat it!"

Gentry frowns. "You needn't sound quite so enthusiastic about the food you'd *like* to eat."

"Sorry."

Rose says, "Your biscuits are divine. And your bacon smells heavenly."

"These two items are all the cooking I know."

Rose smiles. "I could teach you how to make bacon gravy right now. Would you like that?"

Gentry grins and says, "Would *you* like that, Emmett?"

I try to act like I don't care either way, which makes Gentry laugh.

"I'd love you to teach me gravy, Rose."

Scarlett says, "Can I help?"

"Yes, of course!" Gentry says.

After Scarlett gets up to help, I sidle over to see she's drawn a perfect likeness of the outlaw, Bose Rennick, a man she's never laid eyes on in her life. I put that page beneath the others so Gentry won't see it, and find another drawin' of a man's face at the bottom of the stack. It's as good a likeness as you'd ever care to see, but it's a face I don't recognize. And he ain't dressed like a cowboy. He's got long, curly hair, a mustache, a funny hat, and some sort of scarf.

I motion Scarlett over.

"This is an excellent drawin'. Is this someone's face you just made up?"

"No, sir. That's Mr. George."

Gentry walks over, gives the drawin' a careful look. Then shakes her head.

She don't know Mr. George, neither.

CHAPTER 22

AFTER BREAKFAST, ROSE asks our permission to take Scarlett to the river.

Gentry says, "I'll get her chore clothes."

Rose goes outside and comes back a minute later with Scarlett's dress and underclothes.

"As promised," she says.

"How did you *do* that?" Gentry says.

"Washtub, dolly stick, and a little elbow grease."

"You didn't get those stains out with soda crystals."

"No."

"What did you use?"

"An aggressive cleansing agent."

"What's it made from? Wait. How did you manage to *press* the dress without an iron?"

Rose smiles. "So many questions!"

Realizing she's not apt to get a straight answer on the washin', Gentry turns the conversation to the river trip. "I trust you don't intend to store snake excrement in our home."

"I've got a good place already picked out," Rose says.

"Where?"

"Wayne's root cellar."

"Papa calls him Shrug," Scarlett says.

"I know, dear."

"I didn't know Shrug had a root cellar," I say.

"One could write a book about what you don't know about Wayne."

"Like the rumor he can talk? I doubt that's true. He's had lots of chances."

Gentry smiles and shakes her head.

Rose says, "He talks, but rarely with his mouth."

"I ain't familiar with that expression."

"It's not an expression. It's a fact. Has it never occurred to you that Wayne makes a few simple gestures with his hands, but you always know exactly what he's trying to say? Even when it's abstract or complicated?"

"I don't know what abstract means, but Shrug's good at signin' with his hands."

"Right. And when did you ever study signing?"

"The Indians sign all the time."

"Do you understand *them*?"

"No."

But now that she's brought it up I wonder why this never crossed my mind before, the way Shrug and I communicate.

Rose answers the question for me, sayin', "Wayne talks with his mind."

I turn to Scarlett.

"Don't ask *me*," she says. "I'm only three."

Gentry says, "Emmett, since we're on the subject, I'm a little disappointed in Wayne."

"Why?"

"He hasn't bothered to meet the new folks."

"Bothered?"

"Taken the time. Made the effort."

"If I had to make a list of all the folks Shrug hates bein' around, proper city folk would be right at the top, along with wild Indians and outlaws."

"I suppose you're right. But they seem awfully eager to have us go to Philadelphia."

"What are you suggestin'? Have you got a funny feelin' about it?" I put a lot of stock in Gentry's funny feelin's.

She looks at the three of us, lookin' at her. "I'm not suggesting they have an ulterior motive beyond wanting to build the town. I'm just saying they're practically pushing us out the door."

"And?" Rose says.

"And if they're hiding any secrets of ill-will, wouldn't Wayne want to know?"

I grin. "Who's gonna hide secrets from a man who can hear a moth cough when it lights on a rock?"

Rose says, "Gentry? It won't just be Wayne guarding the town. I'll be here, too."

"And me," Scarlett says.

Gentry's lips form a flat smile.

Rose says, "Perhaps we should discuss the real issue."

"What do you mean?" I ask, confused.

"Gentry's concerned when you get back to Dodge, Scarlett will have changed. She's afraid my influence will lead Scarlett to a dark place."

I look at Gentry, then back at Rose. "You wouldn't do that, would you?"

"No."

"Then shouldn't you reassure Gentry?"

"Yes. In fact, I should have done that from the start. Gentry, I hope you know in your heart I would never do anything to turn Scarlett from her parents. I'm only teaching her survival and medical skills."

"Which seems to cover a lot of ground," Gentry says. "As she's fond of saying, she's only three."

"True. But this is the best time to learn."

"And why is that?"

"Because she's glowing."

"You're talking about the condition she has that makes people want to be around her?"

"Yes. But it also opens her up to the mysteries of the world. She'll have the glow for less than half her life. But the best time for learning is now."

Seein' Gentry's frown, Rose adds, "My relationship with Scarlett is similar to my relationship with you."

"How so?"

"Every afternoon, before you leave for Philadelphia, I'll teach you all you can learn about cooking. But no matter how good you get, it won't make you love your family any less. And they'll benefit from your knowledge. It's the same

111

with Scarlett. She's going to learn skills that will benefit the whole family. The whole town, actually."

"Makes sense to me!" I say, thinkin' of all the good cookin' I'm apt to enjoy from here on out. I'm even thinkin' if word gets out that Gentry's learned to cook, some of the county's wild element might go back to stealin' cattle and bustin' heads so I can keep my jail cells full.

Rose says, "I should have made my purpose clearer when I first arrived."

"Why didn't you?" I say.

"I was just so excited to learn how far my godchild had progressed on her own. I knew she'd be smarter than her peers, that was a given. But I hadn't imagined she'd be smarter than...*everyone!*"

CHAPTER 23

"EACH MORNIN' ROSE teaches Scarlett about medicine, and each afternoon she teaches Gentry about cookin'."

Shrug and me are sittin' on the roof of what'll someday be the Dodge City Bank. He's signin' questions he already knows the answers to, but what I've learned about Shrug, it ain't the facts he's after, but my reaction to 'em.

He signs me another question.

I answer, "They're both workin' hard, but Scarlett's makin' the most progress. That ain't to say I'm disappointed with Gentry's cookin'. That stew last night was fine."

He reminds me he was there last night for what Rose called Gentry's *day-byoo*. Then he signs somethin' about 'Nade perch, which causes me to say "Camp cookin's easy. Anyone can fry meat in a pan over an open fire. But indoor stoves and such?" I shake my head.

He explains he wasn't comparin' Gentry's cookin' to outdoor fryin'. He was askin' if me and Gentry planned to do any fishin' on our trip.

As he moves his hands around it dawns on me Rose was right. I ain't readin' his signs, I'm readin' his thoughts. It comes to me for the first time in all the years we've known each other to say, "It'd be a helluva lot easier if you just spoke to me."

"What would you like me to say?"

"Anythin'! Anythin' at all! I mean—wait. Did you just speak to me? Did I just hear your *voice*?"

He signs he has no idea what I'm talkin' about.

"You spoke to me just now. I *heard* you!"

He signs I must have dreamt it.

Before I can argue further, Shrug jumps to his feet and pulls two rocks from his bag. I stand beside him and try to follow his gaze.

"Where?" I say.

He points to the north entrance of town. We're high enough to see two riders slowly approachin'. They appear to be draggin' a large carcass behind 'em, though it ain't stirrin' up much dust.

Shrug puts the rocks back in his bag and lifts an arm as high as he can reach, and waves it back and forth. One of the riders does the same. Then Shrug motions me to climb down with him.

"We're gonna go meet 'em?" I say.

He nods, hops off the roof, and waits for me to climb down. Then he leads me to my horse shed and waits while I saddle Sally.

"Are they just gonna stand out there on the prairie till we get there?"

He nods.

"Who are they? And what's that they're draggin'?"

He grins.

I ride and Shrug bounds behind me. As we get closer I recognize them. One's a horrifyin' giant female accountant, and the other used to be a mule skinner.

"Sadie Nickers!" I say.

She nods. "Emmett. Wayne."

Shrug nods back. Then, to my complete shock, Shrug says, "Hi Ella."

The giant, beastly woman's face breaks into a wide, toothless grin. She hops off her horse and embraces Shrug.

Sadie pats my horse's neck, then leans closer and pats my leg while sayin', "I wish you were that happy to see *me*, handsome."

I back my horse a couple feet away and say, "How're things at the tradin' post?"

"Boomin'!"

"And Jackson Corn's men?"

"Two decided to stay. They're the ones found this unusual horse."

She lifts her chin to indicate the flattened animal I thought was a carcass.

I'd already figured out it was some sort of horse, but..."It's alive?"

"Alive and well."

Sadie watches Shrug and Ella cavort around a minute, then says, "If they start fuckin', I'd like to make use of your pecker, if that'd suit you."

I give her a double look. "Excuse me?"

"You heard me, Sheriff."

"You're mighty direct."

"You mean for a woman?" She laughs. "In my line of work there ain't much time for plantin' rose bushes and waitin' for love to bloom."

"What about the men who work for you?"

She says, "Do you poke your whores?"

"No."

"Because it creates nothin' but trouble and can ruin a good business, right?"

"That, plus I already got a wonderful woman."

"I heard. And a daughter."

"Then you'll understand why I can't—"

"Whoa, Sheriff. I want to dance, not join the band."

"Huh?"

"I have no interest in learnin' to fiddle. I just want to fiddle around."

"I ain't sure what you're sayin', exactly."

"I want a partner for when I feel like dancin'. Someone who just wants the occasional dance. I don't care what he does when he leaves my dance floor."

"You have an unusual way of expressin' yourself," I say.

"You think?"

"I do."

She winks. "Wait till you see how I express myself when I'm nekkid. I'm positively animalistic."

"What's that mean?"

"It means I ain't a town gal. I don't require a feather bed. Don't expect my partner to bathe, or whisper sweet words in my ear. If you've got business in my part of the country I don't care if you've rode six days on a lathered horse with vomit in your beard."

"I ain't got a beard."

"Maybe that's part of the attraction. My point is, if you've got time to cozy up under a blanket, you'll be glad you did. But when you ain't, just bend me over a table for two minutes and save the thank you's till the next time."

"That' a temptin' proposal for any man, and I appreciate the offer. But me and Gentry have somethin' special, and—"

"Spare me. Ain't nothin' worse than a tethered man sayin' he's happy to be tethered. Consider it an open invitation. Southwest Nebraska's a lonely place to camp for the night, and not to brag, but I'm fun company to be with. I *can* be, at least. So next time you set camp in my area on a cold winter's night, take a minute to think about the warm, willin' body waitin' for you at Sadie's Tradin' Post. You can think of Gentry while pokin' *me*, if you like, and even shout her name while in the throes of rapture."

"It's a no for me, Sadie, but that's a helluva fair offer you've made."

"Just wanted you to know how I feel, Sheriff. People come and go so fast in our lives I didn't want to leave any words unsaid. You never know when you meet someone if they might wind up holdin' a special place in your heart.

You watch them ride off and wonder if you should've said somethin'. Most times I don't. But I like you."

"I like you too, Sadie."

Shrug and Ella finally stop gropin' each other long enough for her to walk over and introduce herself. She puts her hand out, spits in it, and says, "Howdy, Sheriff. I'm Ella. Ella Foreskin."

I nod. "Emmett Love. Saw you takin' inventory at Jackson Corn's last week."

"You don't intend to shake my hand?"

"It ain't personal. I don't allow folks to grip my shootin' hand. Can't tell you how many times I've seen a man get shot while another was grippin' his hand."

"You don't trust me."

"Like I say, it ain't personal."

"Do you trust me or not?"

"I don't know you well enough to answer that."

"Are you saying you'd shake my hand if you knew me better?"

"No. I will never shake your hand. Not willin'ly."

"Then it *is* personal."

"You sure you're an accountant and not a lawyer?"

"I'm a bear skinner by trade."

That makes sense. She *looks* like a bear skinner.

"What happened to that horse? It looks like a giant spider."

"It's a gift for Wayne."

Shrug grins, hugs her again, grabs the lead line, and starts walkin' the horse around. He takes time to whisper in its ear, and checks it's feet and mouth and hooves. While he's busy with that, Sadie says, "I heard you're a decent man."

"I try to be."

"I was pleased you didn't try to interfere with my business the other day at the tradin' post. About what happened to Jackson Corn."

"Well, it's out of my jurisdiction."

"You could have claimed otherwise."

I stand on my stirrups and look around. Good thing about Dodge, a good lookout can see someone approachin' from more than a mile in every direction. We're far enough out that the only folks in sight are travelin' the Santa Fe Trail, a half-mile south of us. You'd think they'd all swing by Dodge, just to check it out. But the visitors are few compared to what you'd expect. Maybe because from here the prairie looks as endless as the town looks small.

I sit back in the saddle and ask, "Got any plans for the tradin' post?"

"I aim to build a saloon on the state line," Sadie says. "The front door will face Nebraska, the back door, Kansas."

"Why?"

She grins. "A man wanted in either state can walk in the front door, grab a drink, and walk out the opposite door a free man."

"No offense, but that ain't practical. I mean, there can't be many outlaws with half a brain who'd do that, 'cause if they did, the marshals would start hangin' out at the saloon to wait for 'em to show up. And why spend the money to build a saloon? Couldn't you just serve them outlaws from a tent in either state?"

She laughs. "I don't expect outlaws to use the saloon as a getaway."

"I thought you just said—"

"—It's all about marketing, Emmett. Or advertising, or whatever you want to call it. It's the *story* that counts. Once the word gets out, people will come from miles around to see the place where men *could* walk into a saloon as outlaws and walk out as free men."

I think on it while she adds, "It's like Dodge City. Whoever started Dodge gave it that name because it made the original settlers feel safer since Fort Dodge was close by. Those that started Sweetwater and Lake City knew there weren't no lakes nearby, but settlers hear the name and travel there anyway. When they show up disappointed, the town folk talk 'em into stayin'."

"I s'pect you're right," I say, thinkin' on how the stories about me have already prompted people to move to Dodge from Philadelphia.

Shrug leads the flat horse around some more.

Sadie says, "You'll find I normally side with the Cheyenne."

"You'll find I normally don't," I say. "But I'm against what the soldiers done to Black Kettle."

"I told you that because I wanted you to know where my loyalties lie."

"What's that mean?"

"It means the Cheyenne are my friends, and the Dog Soldiers are my customers. So whatever I tell you has to be held in confidence."

"I can keep a secret."

"I heard that about you," she says, "which is why I'm willin' to tell you the Dog Soldiers are plannin' to steal that big-titted gal everyone's talkin' about."

"Shit. When?"

"Next chance they get. A week, maybe."

"I appreciate the warnin'."

We watch Shrug workin' with the horse.

I'll step right up and declare there ain't a more know-ledgeable horse person on earth than Shrug, but it don't take an expert to see that what he's walkin' around on the lead line is a crushed horse.

"Give him a try!" Ella says, and that's when it hits me the horse has been trampled same as Shrug. And it's low and wide enough that Ella thinks he might be able to ride it.

For the next half-hour we watch Shrug get thrown off this spider-lookin' horse every way a man can be flung, and even some that didn't seem possible till today. But it's clear with each throw Shrug is makin' progress, and by the time Sadie and Ella say their goodbyes, my friend Shrug has a horse he can work with, if not ride.

I climb off Sally to keep Shrug company as he leads his new horse back to town.

"You spoke to Ella," I say. "Out loud. With your voice."

He signs I must have dreamt it.

"Everyone says you can talk. And sing, too. And I heard you talk. Didn't I?"

He signs I must have dreamt it.

"Fine. Be that way."

He laughs.

PART TWO: COACHES AND TRAINS

CHAPTER 24

IT WEREN'T EASY keepin' two secrets from Gentry, but the look on her face tells me the first one was worth keepin'.

That's the one where she's all packed up to go to Philadelphia, but wonders why we ain't hitched a buckboard, and why I insisted on bringin' her to the *Spur* while leavin' our luggage at home.

She's even more surprised upon enterin' the *Spur* to find that all the folks from Old Dodge traveled twelve miles to tell us goodbye and wish us a safe trip. Over the next forty minutes she wonders why the kids from both towns keep peekin' out the front door, but she don't dwell on it, 'cause every few minutes she spies Scarlett, and gives her a hug. And every hug requires tears and a short lecture. The rest of the time she's so besieged by well-wishers, she never thinks to ask me where Shrug is.

Suddenly the kids at the front door holler, "*It's here! It's here!*" When they run outside, squealin' with delight, Gentry realizes somethin' special's happened. Me and the rest of the town's grownups walk her out the front door. When she sees the stage coach, she nearly faints.

"*How on earth!*" she says, over and over.

A 'course we have to wait till all the whores and kids and townspeople climb inside and out, and try both doors and climb on top, and check the wheels and spokes and luggage area, and meet the driver, Dewey Doss. The Philadelphians are amused at all the fuss the town folk are makin', since stagecoaches are second nature to them.

"I've never seen such excitement!" Penelope says. "You'd think President Lincoln was riding in the coach."

"This is the biggest thing that's ever happened in Dodge!" Tom Collins says.

Penelope turns to see who said that, and jumps back in horror. Then tries her best to apologize for bein' rude.

"Don't you worry about it for a minute, pretty Miss," Tom says. "I scare myself worse than I scare other people."

"Have you seen a doctor for your condition?"

"Nope, but I aim to see one today."

"Where?"

He points at Rose.

Penelope says, "Is Rose a midwife?"

"Doctor."

Tom is Old Dodge's retired blacksmith. He's also completely yellow 'cept for his fingers and toes, which are black. He lost an arm and leg in the war. When his skin condition festers he's widely considered the worst-smellin' man in the Kansas territory, apart from the buffalo hunters.

"Emmett?" Penelope says. "Can this be true? A female doctor?"

I nod.

"You introduced her as Scarlett's nanny."

"She's that, too."

"Where did she receive her medical training?"

"I have no idea. But you won't find a better doctor anywhere in the country. Includin' Philadelphia."

"If what you say is true—"

"—It is."

"—This might be the most progressive town in the entire nation!"

"Well, she's just visitin'."

"Would she ever consider moving here?"

"I don't rightly know. Maybe you can talk her into it while we're gone."

She looks around, then lowers her voice. "I'm really going to miss you, Sheriff."

"I'll miss you, too."

She finds my eyes with hers. "Do you understand what I'm saying, Emmett?"

"A 'course I do!"

Her face is flushed. She takes my hand in hers and pulls it toward her. When she does that, it sort of brushes up against her bosom for a second, and I'm glad she don't' seem to notice, 'cause she surely would've been embarrassed. She smiles and says, "I've wanted to tell you this for a long time. You know, about my feelings, and how much I'm going to miss you." She closes her eyes and sighs. Then opens them and says, "I'm so glad I got up the courage to tell you!"

"Me, too," I say, though I don't know why it requires much courage to tell someone they'll be missed.

She gives my hand back, and me and Jim Bigsby head to my house to fetch the luggage.

"She's a looker," he says.

"Who?"

"Penelope."

"You think?"

"She likes you."

"I like her, too."

"You do?"

"A 'course I do! That whole bunch seems like good people."

He makes a clucking sound and says, "Be careful, my friend."

"I will," I say. Then add, "I s'pect the soldiers will stay south of us, and the hostiles north."

He says, "I'm talking about Penelope."

"What about her?"

By then we're at my house. We grab the luggage and start headin' back to the stage coach. Then I remember he'd brought up Penelope's name twice on the way over, and I wonder if maybe he's sweet on her. That wouldn't do, him bein' married to Clara and all.

"What about Penelope?" I ask.

We walk some, and he says, "I wonder how well you understand women."

"The only thing I need to know about women is what makes Gentry happy."

"Well said, Emmett."

As we approach the stagecoach, I notice Penelope wavin' at us while dabbin' her eyes with a handkerchief.

Jim says, "Keep your thoughts on Gentry."

"Why wouldn't I?"

"Just saying."

I give him a long look while we stuff the luggage under the front bench of the coach cab. I hope I'm wrong, but I feel like Jim might be harborin' improper thoughts about Penelope.

CHAPTER 25

THE SECOND SECRET don't go over very well.

That's the one that happens ten miles into our stagecoach ride, when we stop at Alma's Bend, and Gentry sees Shrug and Enorma Stitz standin' outside the way station. At first she's surprised. Then concerned. Then she says, "What's going on, Emmett?"

"I got word the Dog Soldiers were plannin' to steal Enorma."

"When?"

"Next week."

"Why is she *here?*"

"She needed to get the hell out of Dodge. So Shrug snuck her out. Before dawn."

"That much is obvious. But if he's guarding Enorma, who's guarding the town and our daughter?"

"Shrug ain't stayin'. He's headin' back to protect the town."

"When?"

"Directly."

"He's planning to what, just *leave* her here? In this hole-in-the-wall? Emmett, there aren't but three sod houses and a well. She'll be a sitting duck when word gets out." She pauses, then says, "Why are they just standing there, looking so sheepish?"

"What do you mean?"

"Why aren't they coming to greet us?"

"I told 'em to hang back a while, till I had a chance to explain things to you."

"Because you knew this would be a problem for me?"

"Not the part about seein' 'em."

She gives me a close look. "Which part did you think would be a problem, Emmett?"

"The part where you find out Enorma's travelin' with us to Philadelphia."

Gentry stares straight ahead as if in a daze. Then she grabs her carpetbag, shoves it hard into her face, and lets out a muffled scream. Enorma don't seem to hear it, but the stagecoach horses do. They whinny, and try to rear up. Shrug heard it, too. He kicks a dirt clod, and looks away.

I say, "Look, I know it ain't a perfect situation—"

"*Really* Emmett? You're aware it's not a perfect situation? Well, *that's* a good sign, at least."

"I also know she's a neighbor, and you'd feel terrible if she got captured by the Dog Soldiers, who ain't just Indians, but hostiles, come together from different tribes to terrorize settlers. This is a band of the fiercest, angriest renegades on earth. If they were to capture Enorma, she wouldn't live more'n three days. And it wouldn't be a pleasant three days, neither."

Gentry says, "I'm not a cruel person. You know I feel badly for the Stitzes. And no, I don't want Enorma to be captured and brutalized by savages. At the same time, you know how hard it was for me to leave Scarlett for the next four weeks. The *only* thing that kept me going was the idea you and I would have some private time to rekindle our love. I felt I owed you that, since I've been such a poor lover ever since you rescued me from Mr. Wilkins."

"I've got no complaints, though it's true Scarlett's a handful, and you've had a double work load." I put my hand on hers and say, "Truth be told, I was lookin' forward to the two of us bein' alone more than you can imagine. It broke my heart to make this decision."

Gentry's eyes plead with me as she says, "Is there no place for the girl to go besides with us, on our trip?"

"No place safe."

She sighs.

I say, "I'm thinkin' of the girl *and* the town. Harlan and Mary are putin' the word out that Enorma ran off with a union army officer. The Dog Soldiers will hear about it at the tradin' post. They'll probably send a scout or two to sniff around, but in the end they'll see she's gone and bypass Dodge."

"How do you know they'll hear about it at the trading post?"

"I met with the people who run it. They're the ones told me about the Dog Soldiers in the first place. They're also friends of Shrug's, so they'll keep him informed about the hostiles."

It takes a couple more minutes of explainin', but Gentry's a good-hearted woman who loves me deeply, and knows my heart's in the right place. Still, that don't keep her from makin' me ride up top when Enorma enters the coach.

Shrug puts Enorma's small bundle in the coach. The poor girl has almost no extra clothing, and the little she's got is gathered up in a sheet bound together with twine.

"I can put the luggage up top to make more room if we need it," I say, wonderin' if that might make Gentry re-consider our ridin' accommodations.

"We'll be fine," Gentry says.

While the women get settled in the coach, I visit with Shrug.

"No one saw you leave town?"

He shakes his head.

"Enorma rode Gentry's horse?"

He attempts to hide a grin, then turns and motions me to follow. He leads me behind one of the sod houses, where my stallion's tied to a wooden stake, and laughs at the ex-pression on my face.

I say, "If you're waitin' for me to ask how the hell Enorma managed to ride this cursed beast in a north-easterly direction when I can't so much as turn him that way without bein' thrown to the ground, you're wastin' your time!"

He nearly falls to the ground, laughin'.

Not to be outdone, I say, "While we're on the subject of horses, where's yours? How come *you* didn't ride?"

He signs he's too sore from the last attempt, which is such an honest answer I actually feel bad for tryin' to yahoo him about it.

That's the thing about Shrug: he ain't like the rest of us. He don't let pride or embarrassment influence his thoughts, decisions, or reactions. While it's true that no one on earth enjoys teasin' me more'n Shrug does, there ain't a mean bone in his busted-up body. And he's so damn good-natured about his shortcomin's, tryin' to tease him about anythin' always backfires on me.

There just ain't no guile in my friend Shrug.

Now we're starin' at each other the way good friends do when gettin' ready to head in opposite directions. Bein' more'n two feet shorter than me on account of his re-arranged bone structure, he has to reach up to put his hand on my arm. When he does so, he nods, which is his way of reassurin' me the town'll be safe while I'm gone.

I nod back, which is my way of tellin' him I know.

"Thanks for bringin' Enorma," I say. "I reckon if you untie the stallion and slap his ass he'll find his way back to Rose in no time."

We walk back to the coach so he can say goodbye to Gentry. I can tell he's a little skittish about approachin' her, since he knows she's unhappy about Enorma bein' here. Gentry sees it too, and climbs out of the wagon to give him a hug.

She says, "Wayne, you're a good friend. I'm not the least bit upset with you."

He smiles.

"Be safe," she says, "and keep an eye on Scarlett when you can."

He helps her back in the coach and signs for her to have a safe trip. Then he scrambles to the front of the coach so he can watch me climb up and sit beside Dewey. He knows I'm embarrassed about what amounts to payin' money to sit up top, so he changes the subject by pointin to the coach and stretchin' his arms out to represent Enorma's bosoms.

I climb back down and whisper, "Your arms ain't long enough to do 'em justice."

Then I walk to the coach and stand by the window and give Gentry one last look to see if she's changed her mind about where I'll be ridin'. She don't, so I climb back up and take my place beside Dewey, who says it's an honor to have Sheriff Love ridin' shotgun for him. We wave a last goodbye to Shrug and start headin' to Wilbur, where we'll bed for the night. Tomorrow we'll spend the night in Kansas City, and from there we'll ride a series of trains all the way to Philadelphia.

As we put Alma's Bend behind us, Dewey says, "That gal in the coach."

"What about her."

"She related to you?"

"Nope. Just a neighbor."

"What did you say her name was?"

"Enorma."

"Enorma what?"

"Stitz."

I wait for him to laugh or accuse me of tellin' tales. But he just nods and says, "She's aptly named." We ride another mile or two and he says, "I reckon she could breast-feed Texas."

CHAPTER 26

"I'M REAL SORRY to be such a burden," Enorma tells Gentry.

"It's not your fault, Enorma. The sheriff's obliged to keep you safe."

They travel a mile over the bumpy terrain in silence, save for the occasional gasp of pain when they hit a particularly hard bump.

"This is very exciting," Enorma says, "but I fear I'll be quite bruised by the time we get to Wilbur."

Gentry smiles. "Let's don't tell Emmett that."

"Why not?"

"I've always wanted to ride in a stagecoach, and Emmett always warned me I'd find it quite painful."

"And you don't want him to say 'I told you so?'"

"Exactly."

"What will you say?"

"I'll tell him it was like riding on a cloud."

Enorma laughs. "That'll be fun. But how will you hide the bruises from him tonight?"

Gentry gives her a look meant to discourage further conversation about the possibility of Emmett seeing the bruised parts of her body. Unfortunately, Enorma fails to grasp the meaning of Gentry's look. Worse, it seems to have caused her mind to dwell on the thoughts Gentry was trying to avoid. This, she determines when Enorma says, "What's it like, Miss Gentry?"

"What's *what* like?"

"Spreading your legs for every miner and cowhand who's got six dollars in his pocket?"

"I beg your *pardon?*" Gentry says, eyes ablaze.

"I just meant, I know it's good money, but is it a good *life?* I mean, would it be a good life for *me?*"

Gentry studies the girl's innocent expression and comes to the conclusion Enorma's ill-chosen words weren't intended to offend. She decides Enorma's been raised by proper parents to be a proper girl, and has no idea former whores like Gentry don't discuss the details of their profession in such a casual manner. And never to proper women. Still, Enorma seems to have been considering prostitution, and Gentry's in the business.

"It's a hard life, Enorma."

"But the money?"

"The money's good. Why do you ask?"

Enorma pauses before saying, "Some of the men in town have offered to pay me to fornicate."

Gentry raises an eyebrow. "Did you mean to say men? Or were you talking about boys?"

"Both."

"Who?"

"I probably shouldn't say."

"How much were you offered?"

"I probably shouldn't say. But I know the going rate is six dollars."

"And?"

"I've been offered way more."

Gentry says, "I'm going to ask you a question you don't have to answer."

Enorma says, "I know what you're going to ask. The answer's no. I've never been with a man. Except that..."

"Except what?"

"I don't like the way Harlan's been looking at me since I...um..."

"Blossomed?"

"Yes, ma'am."

Enorma starts to cry. Gentry tries to calm her, but backs off, realizing the crying has to run its course.

"I've been cursed!" she says, between snuffles. "It's awful! I just wish I were normal!" She adds, "I hate being like this, Miss Gentry, but there's nothing I can do about it." She snuffs some more. "The men in town make fun of me and give me horrible, lustful looks. And every day the women seem to hate me more and more. And now Emmett—"

"Sheriff Love—"

"Sheriff Love says that two Indian tribes want to kidnap me. It's clear I'll never be able to live a normal life, so I was wondering if I should try whoring. If men are going to act crazy around me, or always lust after me, maybe I could turn it to my advantage."

"Not in Dodge, you can't."

"Why not?"

"The town would never stand for it."

"Why?"

"Your family lives there."

"So?"

"I can't go around hiring girls to whore in the same town where their parents live. It would be a threat to every parent in town."

"Why?"

"Use your head, Enorma! How ashamed and furious would your parents be if they heard you were selling your body to their neighbors, friends, and relatives? And if you started earning your own money and buying clothes and other items, how long would it take for the other girls in town to decide if *they* should whore?"

"Wouldn't that be good for your business?"

"It'd be terrible!" Gentry says. "The whole structure of the town, what I call the balance, would collapse. There'd be constant gun battles between horny cowboys and angry fathers. It won't work."

Enorma thinks about it a minute, then says, "I suppose I could move to a big city, like Philadelphia, and sell myself."

The conversation stops while she and Gentry bounce around inside the coach like marbles in a box. When they hit a smooth patch of trail, Enorma says, "If I want to whore, how should I go about getting myself broken in?"

Gentry shakes her head. "I can't believe we're discussing these issues."

"It's just you and me, Miss Gentry. And these are issues I can't discuss with anyone else I know."

"True, but if you tell your parents what I've already said—"

"You don't have to worry about that. If you won't hire me, I'm not going back."

"Why not?"

She laughs. "In case you didn't notice, I'm wearing an old sheet for a blouse. We're the poorest family in town, reduced to handouts. My mother resents me because her husband covets my body. My brother Ben—the only person in the world who loves me—is dying of consumption. The town women hate me, and the men want to rape me. And even if I *do* manage to keep the men and boys off me it won't matter because sooner or later the Indians will get me."

"Maybe you could learn a trade in Philadelphia."

"I can barely read or write! Do you honestly think I could compete for work with city girls my age? And if so, do you know of any work I could attempt that would put immediate dollars in my purse? And is there any trade that would pay me even close to what I could earn by whoring?"

"Well..."

"Make no mistake, Miss Gentry, I hate my body. But men seem to desire it above all sensibility. It seems to me I might as well profit from their lustful weakness."

Gentry sighs. Much as she hates to admit it, Enorma's got a point. With her natural endowments she could easily make a hundred dollars a day in a large city or mining camp.

141

"My real question," Enorma says, "is how to find the right man to break me in. What type of man should I seek?"

"A kind, tender, gentle man. One who respects you."

She frowns. "That doesn't sound like any of the men I know."

They ride in silence a while, then Enorma says, "Do you think Emmett might be willing to break me in, sexually?"

Gentry's face clouds.

Enorma says, "I'd consider it the highest honor."

"You would, huh?"

"Yes, ma'am. An honor."

"How nice."

"Would you ask him for me?"

"No."

Enorma nods. "You're right. That's the sort of thing I should ask him myself. But do you think he'd be willing?"

"To take your virginity?"

"Yes, ma'am."

"Let me put it this way, Enorma: if I ever find out he's willing, I can assure you he won't be able."

She lifts her skirt, removes a derringer from her thigh holster, aims it between Enorma's eyes, and cocks it.

Enorma screams.

Gentry aims the barrel out the window and fires a shot. The stagecoach skids to a stop. Emmett jumps to the ground, hits hard, rolls, and scrambles to his feet, losing his hat in the process. He runs to the coach window and yells, "What's happened?"

"You and Enorma are going to change places."

CHAPTER 27

"THERE'S WRITTEN RULES to ridin' a stagecoach," Dewey says. "And not shootin' out the windows is one of 'em."

He gathers the three of us into a group and pulls a list from his coat.

"I won't bore you with all the flowery language," he says, "but it's clear I should a' called these out to you before we left Dodge, so listen up. Rule number one: when sittin' three to a seat you each get fifteen inches. It ain't much, but keep to your space. Two: if you drink, share the bottle. Three: pipes and cigars are forbidden in the presence of women. Chewin's permitted, but spit *with* the wind, not agin' it. Four: no cussin' in the presence of women and children. Five: guns are permitted and can be used in the event of an attack, but cannot be fired for pleasure or shootin' at wild animals. Six: never jump from the coach, even when dealin' with runaway horses. Seven: stage coach ridin's the bumpiest form of travel known to man. But gents who use the bumps as an opportunity to become overly familiar with female passengers will be put off the coach and forced to walk. Any questions?"

We take our places in and on the coach and continue ridin' to Wilbur. An hour into the journey the sky darkens.

"What on earth?" Gentry says.

I look out the window. "Uh oh."

"What's wrong?"

"Pigeons."

"Pigeons?"

"Yep. And lots of 'em."

"Is that bad?"

"Ever heard of a locust swarm?"

"Of course."

"Passenger pigeons are fifty times larger, and their swarms a million times bigger. But the worst part?"

"Tell me."

"They're nonstop shitters."

Gentry frowns. "You know what I think?"

"What's that?"

"I think you like saying the word 'shit.' You know it rankles me, and you say it anyway."

"When this swarm passes you can offer up a better word if you like. In the meantime we better use them blankets to cover the windows."

She studies my face. "You look like you have more to say."

"I do. I'm not sure what passed between you and Enorma, but it's not going to be very pleasant up top."

Gentry tries to hide an evil smile. "For how long?"

"Days."

"*What?*"

"I've seen pigeons pass overhead for three days and nights without lettin' up. In numbers so thick they blot out the sun."

"That's ridiculous."

"Would you consider lettin' her come in the cabin with us?"

"Are you sure she's likely to get dung on her from these pigeons?"

"It's a certainty."

"How about we give her five minutes up there to learn her lesson."

"She must've really upset you."

"Why, because I'm willing to let her get hit with a little bird poo?"

"It won't be a little. It'll be a lesson she won't soon forget."

"That's a good thing. When will they arrive?"

"You make it sound like guests are comin' to our house for dinner."

She shrugs.

I say, "They'll arrive here directly. They'll start slow, a few hundred at first, but within minutes there'll be thousands. In a half-hour, millions. Then billions. Then...whatever number comes after billions."

"Trillions?" She laughs. "Oh, Emmett, please!"

"What?"

"How gullible do you think I am?"

"I don't rightly know. But when them pigeons come at us by the billions and trillions the noise from their wings will hurt your ears. A few days of that and you'll think the world's comin' to an end. If it lasts as long as I've seen, we might have to put the horses down."

"Why?"

"The noise from the wings will drive 'em crazy."

"You mean it will annoy them."

"I mean it will make them insane. So insane we might have to put them down to end their misery."

She frowns. "You're making this up. How much noise could pigeons possibly make by flapping their wings?"

"I s'pect you'll hear the screams before you hear the wings."

She laughs. "Screaming pigeons?"

"Not the pigeons. Enorma and Dewey."

"Dewey?"

I want to tell her what she can't seem to understand: how in a few hours the entire prairie will be white with pigeon shit. But some things have to be seen to be believed.

I cover the window with a blanket.

She says, "If it's going to be *that* bad, why not cover the other window?"

"Dewey and Enorma will be joinin' us directly."

"Who's going to drive the stagecoach?"

I give her a look. "You really have no idea what's about to happen, do you? I can flat guarantee you that Dewey's already lookin' for a place to tie the horses. When this hits—"

"Wait! What was that horrible sound?"

"The first of Enorma's screams."

But it weren't the last.

The girl has a prodigious set of lungs, and for the next two minutes her screams sound like a platoon of cyclones. Dewey stops the coach. Ten seconds later Enorma comes flyin' in the cabin, covered head to toe in pigeon shit. She looks like she's been dunked in a barrel of white glue. Or like a snow woman, startin' to melt, except that what's oozin' from her hair and slidin' thickly down her face is pigeon shit. She's huffin' and cryin' and shakin' like a leaf.

"*I hope you're happy!*" she screams at Gentry.

Gentry ain't happy.

She's startin' to get worried.

'Cause if Enorma looks this bad after two minutes, and the pigeons ain't started arrivin' in big numbers yet...

I climb out and help Dewey secure the horses. Then he and I join the girls in the coach and block the other window.

"How bad is it, Dewey?" Gentry asks.

"I've seen worse."

"What does *that* mean?"

"Means it's bad, but I've seen worse. Of course, it's just started, which means this one could be the worst."

"Is there nothing we can do but sit here and wait?"

"It's the thing I'd recommend."

The cabin's already ripe with the aroma of pigeon shit. In the hours to come it'll get unbearable for the women.

"I hate Dodge City," Enorma says. "But I wish I was back there now."

"What about Wayne?" Gentry says.

I give her a look to show I'm right pleased she thought to worry about Shrug at a time like this, when most women would be quite upset for themselves.

"He'll find a creek somewhere and hunt for a animal burrow in one of the river banks."

"And if he can't find one?"

"He'll scoop one out big enough to hold him. River bank ground is generally soft in April. It's a good place to weather the swarm."

"Why is that a good place?"

"He'll have water to drink, and plenty to eat."

"What will he eat?"

"Pigeons."

She frowns. "What if he can't find a creek?"

"Then he'll have to lie down and cover up under some blankets. But the good news is he'll still have plenty to eat."

Two hours later, the interior cabin is dark as dusk. Though we're inside, the noise of pigeon wings fills our ears and grows so loud it drives all thoughts from our heads except the hope that it'll stop.

Two hours after that, the horses start kickin' and shriekin'.

An hour after that, they break away from their tethers and run off.

"That ain't good," I say.

CHAPTER 28

I MOVE THE blanket an inch from the window to see if there's any sign of the swarm lettin' up, but it's darker outside than it is in the cabin.

I wonder how that can be. I mean, we're inside, so it should be darker than the outside, right?

Some things don't make sense.

At any rate, it ain't so dark outside that I can't see what looks like a blizzard of bird shit fallin' to the ground.

"How bad is it?" Gentry asks.

"Not as bad as it will be," I say.

"How is that possible?"

"Because it's just gettin' started."

"I need to pee," Enorma says.

"We all need to pee, Enorma!" Gentry says, with some edge to her voice. Then she says, "I'm sorry, Emorna. I shouldn't have snapped at you. It's not your fault you need to pee."

"I could take the blanket off one of the windows," I say. "Then you gals could go outside one-at-a-time and drape it over yourselves and do your business."

Gentry says, "While we're out there the open window will cause the cabin to foul that much worse."

Dewey says, "I'm sorry, Miss. Most of the new coaches have windows over the door. But since Dodge ain't on our regular route, this is the only coach I could get for your surprise."

I tell Dewey he did a fine job. Then add, "If we didn't have this coach we'd be on horseback right now."

Enorma says, "We don't have to remove a blanket from one of the windows. We can cover ourselves up with the sheet my clothes are wrapped up in."

"Why, that's a fine idea!" Gentry says. "Thank you! And in return, when we get to Kansas City I'll buy you a proper suitcase."

"Really?"

"I promise."

We spend an uncomfortable night in the tiny stage coach, glad to have the shelter. The birds continue passin' over us by the millions hour after hour.

Around noon I say, "I don't believe it!"

"What?" Gentry says.

"We got lucky. It's taperin' off."

"We must've got the light side of the swarm," Dewey says.

"You can't possibly mean that," Gentry says. "The sky was black with birds for more than twenty hours." She peeks out the window. "It's *still* black with birds!"

"But it's lettin' up," Dewey says. "If you listen closely you can hear it ain't as bad as it was a few minutes ago."

"It's *deafening*!" Enorma says.

Gentry says, "You're both right. It's deafening, but less so than it was. How much longer till it's over?"

"Couple hours."

"Thank God!"

"Think the horses'll come back?" I ask.

"They should," Dewey says. "They're my personal stock. I doubt they went far."

He's right. By the time Dewey and I start huntin' for 'em, they show up on their own. We hitch 'em and continue the trip to Wilbur without further incident with Enorma and me ridin' in the cabin. When we get to the way station, Enorma runs to the well and starts pumpin' the handle till the water pours over her head. She works her fingers through her hair for ten full minutes, till the pigeon shit is completely gone. Then she goes in one of the sod houses and changes into her other gown-like dress and comes back out and painstakin'ly washes her soiled duds.

Gentry watches me watchin' her work.

"You seem fascinated by her."

"I am."

"Tell me why."

"She's only got two outfits, and they're the sorts of outfits others would toss away. But she takes pride enough to keep 'em clean. I admire that."

151

"You've got a good heart, Emmett."

"So do you."

"Not like yours."

As we watch Enorma work, she looks up at us. And smiles.

"She's got a nice smile," Gentry says.

I think so too, but decide not to comment on it.

That night, as we bed down on the floor of the way station, Gentry asks if I might happen to have any other types of feelin's for Enorma aside by my fascination for her work ethic.

"What other type of feelin's would I have?"

"What type do you *think*?" she says.

"The only feelin's I got is to keep her safe. Why?"

"She's got a schoolgirl crush on you. No, it's more than that."

"Really?"

"Careful how you say that."

"Are you jealous?"

"Of course not. You're a grown man. You can do what you like."

"I'll be damned!"

"What?"

Part of me is pleased she's jealous, but the rest of me don't like her bein' upset. But she clearly is. One thing I know is this ain't a time for makin' fun of her for it. This is a time for reassurin' her how I feel. So I say, "Gentry, you're the only woman I've wanted since the day we met. And the only one I've touched since then, or ever *will* touch, as long as you'll have me."

"What about May Gray?" she says.

"What about her?"

"The whole town knows the story of how she pulled your pecker in her parlor."

"It was her kitchen."

"Thanks for clearing that up. Now I won't have to get tongue-tied next time I bring it up."

"You shouldn't bring it up at all."

"I can't help it. We live twelve miles apart. And someday soon we'll be living on the same street. Do you have any idea how embarrassing that will be for me?"

"More embarrassing for her, I s'pect."

"Why her, more than me?"

I sigh. "Gentry?"

"What?"

"I told you a hundred times that incident with May was a complete misunderstandin'. We discussed this more'n once, and each time you said you understood. Not to mention you were married to David Wilkins at the time it happened."

"This isn't just about her pulling your pecker. I'm simply saying that whenever you claim you haven't touched another woman since meeting me, you always forget about May."

"That's because I didn't touch her. She touched me."

"That's splitting hairs, don't you think?"

"It's not like you to be this way."

She's quiet a long time. Then says, "You're right. I'm sorry, Emmett." After a brief pause she says, "It'd be different if I hadn't left Scarlett for the first time ever, and if it was just you and me alone on this trip, and if Enorma wasn't so young and didn't have the world's biggest bosoms."

"You don't have to worry about me and Enorma. You're the only woman I'll ever love."

"I believe that, and I trust you. My problem isn't your love, it's her lust. She wants to whore."

"*What?*"

"When we get to Philadelphia."

"You're serious?"

"I am. And worse, she wants you to break her in."

"What does *that* mean?"

"She wants you to take her virginity."

"*What?* She *told* you that?"

"She did. And she's got serious heat in her loins."

"What's that mean?"

"It means she's primed and ready and on the lookout for a man."

"She ain't but fourteen!"

"Emmett, that girl's throwing off more heat than a prairie fire at a Fourth of July picnic."

"Shit!"

"Where are you going?"

"To get Enorma."

"*Why?*"

"Dewey."

"Oh."

Enorma ain't pleased when I drag her away from holdin' hands with Dewey, and even less pleased when I tell her it's time to make her pallet and go to bed. But she's downright angry about havin' to sleep next to Gentry.

But angry as she is, she don't hold a candle to how angry Gentry is.

I fall asleep thinkin' it's gonna be a long-ass trip to Philadelphia with these two women.

A couple hours later, when it's pitch black in the way station, Enorma whispers, "Emmett? Would you escort me to the outhouse?"

Before I can answer I hear the distinctive click of a derringer bein' cocked.

Enorma says, "On second thought, I can hold it till morning."

"Good decision," I say.

CHAPTER 29

THANKFULLY, KANSAS CITY improves the girls' moods. Between the stores, shops, restaurants, and hotels, there just ain't enough time or energy for hard feelin's.

In my experience, few things in life will put a faster step in a woman's stride, or a brighter smile on her face than a new store and a purse full of money. Since all the money we have these days is technically Gentry's, her forgivin' nature and generous heart shines through as she insists on loadin' Enorma up with real, store-bought clothes—the first she's owned in eight years.

The sights and sounds of Kansas City on a sunny Saturday in April are bringin' Enorma and Gentry together like a narrow blanket on a winter buggy ride. They're havin' such a good time shoppin', Gentry asks if we can stay another day to see the parks and landmarks.

I'm thrilled to say yes.

We get up early Sunday mornin', catch a church service that features pipe organ music and a two-hour service instead of the one they advertised, and spend most of the day walkin' through the parks and public gardens. We cap off a long day of sightseein' with a visit to the State Capitol, which ain't too far from our hotel, the Claiborne-McCallum, on State Street. We go straight up to the room so the girls can get spiffed up in their new clothes for dinner, and plan to eat early 'cause our train leaves at seven-thirty tomorrow mornin'.

The room we're stayin' in has a parlor *and* a bedroom, which is pretty highfalutin for an old mud boot like me. It's about four-thirty Sunday afternoon, April 9th, and I'm stretched out on the bed while Gentry's takin' a bath in a real bathtub down the hall. When she comes back, Enorma's gonna take her turn.

I'm half asleep when I hear Enorma call me from the parlor.

I get up and stand by the door that connects the two rooms.

"You okay?"

"I need your help."

I hesitate a minute, mindful of what Gentry said to me a couple nights ago, about how Enorma's givin' off heat.

"What's wrong?"

"I want to get your opinion of the dress I was planning to wear to dinner."

"Gentry's opinion would be sounder," I say.

"I know, but I've already put it on. Do you think it's fancy enough for the restaurant we're going to?"

That question seems harmless enough. I open the door and see Enorma standin' ten feet away, holdin' up one a' her new dresses.

"That looks like a fine choice," I say.

She grins and says, "Oops!"

...And lets the dress fall to the floor.

At which point I can't help but notice she's one hundred percent naked.

Which turns out to be the moment Gentry does *not* enter the room.

But I s'pect she will, any second.

I'm flustered, nervous, and tryin' not to look at what's right there in front of me, and it slowly dawns on me that the best way not to see it is to cover my eyes, turn, and leave the room. However long it took me to come to that realization is the only amount of time I stared at her nakedness. But when I cover my eyes and start to turn, she says, "Sheriff!"

I look up, and she's comin' right at me.

"Get dressed right this second, or I'll tell Gentry!"

"No!"

"What did you say?"

She tosses her head and runs past me, jumps on the bed, and sprawls out. "What a nice bed!" she says. "I think I'll wait right here till Miss Gentry comes back."

"Enorma, stop foolin' around. This ain't no game. Gentry will flat shoot you. Don't think she won't. Now put some clothes on and get your ass back in the parlor."

"No."

"Is that your last word on the subject?"

"It is."

"I'll apologize right now for what I'm about to do."

"You're forgiven," she says. "Now, come and get it, cowboy."

"That ain't the plan," I say.

I grab my gun, point it at her, and cock the hammer.

"You wouldn't!"

"I will. Last chance. Get up and get dressed or I'll shoot you."

"Shoot away, Sheriff, as I don't believe you for a second."

She opens her arms like she's tryin' to hug me from where she's lyin'. I take that opportunity to shoot her hand. She lets out a blood-curdlin' scream.

Then all hell breaks loose.

Gunfire suddenly erupts in the street below our window. Hundreds of guns are shootin' at the same time. It's like the war has caught up to downtown Kansas City and a major street battle's takin' place. Enorma's shriekin' and carryin' on like she's dyin', but I aimed well. It ain't no more than a scratch. She ain't the first woman I've shot between the thumb and forefinger, and probably won't be the last. So I've got that shot down pretty well. Last time I shot a woman, I split the web of her hand. In Enorma's case, I barely creased it. She'll need a bandage, but she'll be fine in a day or two if she don't let it get infected.

Meanwhile the gunfire outside is escalatin'.

I bust the glass out of the parlor window in case I need to defend myself.

Enorma screams for me to come back and help her. I get a good look at what's happenin' on the street and come to the conclusion I ain't witnessin' a battle, but some sort of celebration, instead. Hundreds of people are pourin' onto the street, huggin' each other and squeezin' off shots.

I wonder what's got 'em so excited, but can't take the time to deal with it right now, 'cause I got a bigger problem.

Gentry.

I can't imagine what might happen if she catches Enorma in my bed, naked, with blood on the spread.

I holler, "Stop carryin' on! I barely scratched you with that bullet. Now listen up: I'm headin' to fetch Gentry. I'll leave it to you to explain what happened here. But if you're still naked when I get back, I'll not stop her from shootin' you."

I go out the door and down the hall, callin' Gentry's name. By then cannon fire shakes the walls and foundation of the hotel. That, plus the shootin' and hollerin' from the lobby and street below is pure pandemonium.

From inside the bathroom Gentry yells, "Are we under attack?"

"No. It's some sort of celebration."

"You sure?"

"Positive. Are you okay?"

"Yes. Is Enorma okay?"

"I just left her."

"Good. Will you stand guard while I get dressed?"

"A' course."

I wait till she comes out.

She says, "Can you go downstairs and find out what's going on?"

"Sure."

I turn, but don't get far before Enorma comes out the room, fully dressed, yellin', "I just heard! The war's over! General Lee surrendered!"

"Your hand!" Gentry says. "What happened?"

"I got shot!"

"*What?*"

"It's just a scratch. They're shootin' guns all over the place outside. A bullet came flying through the window and hit me in the hand!"

"You poor thing!" she says.

She runs to Enorma's side and says, "Let me see."

Enorma shows her, and Gentry hauls off and slaps her across the face.

Enorma screams and starts runnin' back to the room. Gentry follows. I follow Gentry.

Now we're all in the room and Enorma's swearin' her story's true.

But she underestimates Gentry.

"Here's the window they shot through," Enorma says.

"That's too big for a bullet hole," Gentry says.

"The glass must've shattered."

"Except there's no glass on the floor."

Gentry checks the bedroom. "Where's the spread?"

"I grabbed it to stop the bleeding."

"Enorma—"

"I swear!"

Gentry looks at me, holds her palm out.

I hand over my gun.

She checks the cylinder, spies the missing bullet, turns the gun on Enorma and says, "I'll give you the count of three to tell the truth."

Enorma says, "I didn't want to get him in trouble."

"Who?"

"Emmett."

"What're you trying to say?"

"Emmett came for me. Said he was going to break me in. I couldn't stop him. The truth is, I didn't want to." She looks at me and says, "Thank you, Emmett. I'm a little sore, but you were perfect." She turns back to Gentry and says, "We did it on the bed. When the celebrating started outside, he was afraid you'd come running in, so he shot my hand and ran to get you."

"And the window?"

"I busted it out to make up the story."

"Because you didn't want to get Emmett in trouble."

"Yes, ma'am. I'm sorry, Emmett."

Gentry looks at me and says, "I'm done with this bitch."

She counts out two hundred dollars, gives it to Enorma, and says, "There are at least twenty whorehouses in this city. Probably one within a block of here. I'll trust you to find it. Now gather your things and get out."

"You can't leave me on my own in this huge city! I'm just a child!"

"You're four years past the age of consent, and two years past the legal age for marriage. You weren't acting like a child in the stagecoach when we left Alma's Bend, and you sure as hell weren't acting like a child a few minutes ago

when you were doing whatever you were doing with
Emmett. Get your things together."

"No. You're responsible for me. You have to take care
of me."

Gentry points my gun at her face. "I *will* kill you. I'll kill
you and blame it on the gunfire below."

"You wouldn't dare."

Gentry cocks the hammer.

"You wouldn't *dare!*" Enorma yells.

Gentry says, "Goodbye, Enorma!" and pulls the trigger.

CHAPTER 30

THE SOUND FROM the gun was a click instead of a gunshot.

That's 'cause Gentry had the foresight to turn the cylinder back to the round I spent when shootin' Enorma's hand. But the look on Gentry's face convinces Enorma to start packin' her clothes anyway.

While she does so she shouts, "You people are *crazy!* You're *insane!*"

"You lied," Gentry says. "I can't abide a liar."

"Fine. I lied. Okay? But the God's honest truth is Emmett saw me naked. He saw every inch of me naked."

Gentry cocks the hammer.

"I swear to God!" Enorma says. "Ask him. He'll tell you."

"I don't need to ask him what happened. He shot you. That's good enough for me."

"He saw me *naked!*" she screams.

"I'm happy for him." She looks at me. "I'm guessing they were big, right? It's okay, you can say."

"Big ain't the word."

"Try for the right word, Emmett."

"Really big."

"That's two words."

"Well, there were two of 'em."

She nods.

Enorma says, "What'll you tell my parents? They *trusted* you. *I* trusted you."

"Emmett and I will tell them the truth. And don't forget, you already announced your intention to stay in Philadelphia, so you may as well stay here. You also said Harlan was making eyes at you and your mother resented you for it."

"What about my brother, Ben?"

"We're not banishing you from the town, Enorma. You can go there tomorrow, live there, visit there...you've got options."

"What about the Indians?"

They look at me to answer that.

I say, "If the war's truly over, a lot of these soldiers will be lookin' for work. I s'pect the government will pay 'em to fight Indians. Still, if I was you, I'd stay out of the Kansas Territory for the next two or three years. There will be bloodshed."

Enorma starts cryin' again. She finishes packin' and says, "I can't believe you're doing this. You're *responsible* for me!"

Gentry says, "In the stage coach you asked how much you could earn by whoring. The truth is you'd get top dollar. I'm not sure what that means in Philadelphia, but here in Kansas City a girl like you could make two hundred a night at the right brothel. But look at me, Enorma."

She does.

"You don't have to whore. The two hundred dollars I gave you will get you back to Dodge with plenty left over to help your family. Or it can get you set up nicely right here in Kansas City. You can clerk, teach school, cook in a restaurant, or apprentice at some other trade. You're young. Pretty. You've got money, and a suitcase full of clothes. You've got options. That's more than I had when I was your age. Goodbye, Enorma."

Enorma looks at me with pleadin' eyes. "Emmett?"

"What?"

"*Say* something!"

"Goodbye, Enorma," I say. "And good luck."

She spends a couple minutes sobbin', and twice that long beggin' Gentry's forgiveness. When neither works, she picks up her suitcase and leaves.

When the door closes, I say, "You think she'll be all right?"

"I know she will. Trust me, that girl will get whatever she wants in life. She'll probably...Give me a minute."

Gentry goes out the door and stays gone a long time. When she comes back she says, "I can be ready for dinner in twenty minutes. Will that suit you, Sheriff? Or would you prefer to see *me* naked first?"

"You naked first."

She grins.

I've heard it said there are probably ten days in a person's life he or she will never forget. I reckon I'll never forget where I was and what I was doin' the moment I learned the war ended. But the rest of the night turned out to be just me and Gentry, in a feather bed, which was even more memorable than all the rest.

CHAPTER 31

GENTRY AND I missed plenty of meals on the prairie before, so skippin' dinner weren't a hardship for either of us.

Havin' said that, the complete truth about last night is we couldn't have eaten if we wanted to, 'cause all the cooks and waiters ran off to celebrate General Lee's surrender. The bar was open, though, so I bought a bottle of whiskey and brought it up to the room to continue our own, personal celebration.

I poured us a drink and said, "You were gone a long time after Enorma left. What' happened?"

We took a sip. "This is really sweet," she said.

"It ought to be! It was four dollars!"

She laughed. "That's crazy."

"It's a celebration. So what happened between you and Enorma?"

"I took her to the front desk and got her a room and pre-paid it for a month."

"Out of the two hundred you gave her?"

"No. I let her keep the full two hundred."

I shook my head. "You're a hell of an understandin' woman."

"Not really. But I felt responsible for making sure she was safe."

"You helped her get settled in?"

"I did."

"You talked to her about whorin'?"

Gentry sighed. "She's dead set on it, so I told her how to find the right brothel and madam, what to look for, how to protect herself. Those sorts of things."

"If she's gonna whore, why'd you get her the hotel room?"

"I told Enorma she didn't have to whore or find a job at all, if she didn't want to, since we'd be back in three to four weeks to check on her. I said if she wasn't happy here for any reason, and wanted to go back to Dodge, we'd take her with us."

I smiled. "You're not so tough."

"No?"

"I will admit you had me fooled for a minute."

"How so?"

"When you fired the empty chamber I thought you meant to shoot her."

"I did."

"What do you mean?"

"I didn't turn the cylinder to the empty chamber on purpose. It just happened."

"You thought you were shootin' her?"

"I did."

"Wow."

"I know."

"Are you glad you didn't?"

She thought about it a minute. "Did she pull your pecker?"

"Nope. I had my clothes on the whole time."

"Then yes. I'm glad I didn't shoot Enorma."

"It took you a while to answer," I said.

"That's because if I have to see her in Dodge it'll be hard on me. Every time I see her I'll remember you saw her naked. It's bad enough having to be civil to May Gray." She paused. "Is there anyone else I have to worry about seeing in Dodge who's made a pass at you?"

"Sadie Nickers."

"Who the hell is *that*?"

"Former mule skinner I met at the tradin' post."

"You saw *her* naked, too?"

"Nope. But she offered."

She frowned. "For an old man you sure get a lot of action."

"I was thinkin' the same thing myself. A little while ago. When I was with you."

"Want a little more action?"

"That, or a *lot* more!"

Moments later, under the covers, she said, "Sadie Nickers?"

"Uh huh."

"Nickers? Like the underwear fancy ladies wear in Europe?"

"I guess, though Sadie don't strike me as the fancy underwear type."

"Why's that?"

"She's tougher than a burlap chicken!"

"I'm tough, too. Maybe I'll shoot her, as well."

"I'd best keep the two a' you apart, then."

"It's all right. I'm not worried about losin' you to a former mule skinner."

"You shouldn't be worried about losin' me to anyone."

"Too late."

"What do you mean? You can't mean Enorma!"

"Nope."

"Well...certainly not May Gray!"

"Nope."

"Who's left?"

"Penelope."

"What?"

"You heard me."

"But...She's *married*!"

"She's the one."

"What one?"

"A woman in love always recognizes the woman who can replace her."

"I have no idea what you're talkin' about."

"When a woman loves a man as much as I love you, it's a natural thing to notice how other women look at you. And easy to identify the one who could make me lose everything."

"You're sayin' Penelope could make me stop lovin' you?"

"That's what I'm saying."

"That's ridiculous."

"Is it? You don't find her pretty?"

"This discussion's silly."

"You didn't answer me."

"You know who's pretty, Gentry? You! You're the prettiest woman I ever saw. And the second prettiest ain't Penelope, neither. It's Rose. But you ain't afraid of losin' me to Rose, even though we traveled thousands of miles together and camped out at night."

"Like I say, a woman can tell. Rose isn't the one. But Penelope? That's a whole different story."

"There ain't no story to it. She's married, period. And even if she weren't, she ain't you. You're the only woman I want. End of story."

"Thank you, Emmett."

"For what?"

"Saying the words I needed to hear."

Later, in the middle of the night, Gentry woke me up and said, "You seem to put more stock into being married than I realized."

"What do you mean?"

"Every time I mentioned Penelope's name, the first thing you said was 'she's married.'"

"Well, she is."

"You make it sound like some sort of shield. Like her marriage is the wall that keeps you and her apart."

"My love for *you* is the wall that keeps me and her apart. And it ain't just Penelope. It's *all* women."

She kissed my cheek. "You've often said you'd like to marry me."

"Yes."

"Did you mean it?"

"A 'course I meant it."

"Will you?"

"Wait. Are you askin' me to marry you?"

"Yes."

I laughed. "Ain't I supposed to be the one to ask?"

"You asked me a hundred times. Can't I ask *you*, just this once?"

"Yes, but I think the only reason you want to get married is to protect your interests."

"Can you think of a better reason?"

"I don't need a better reason. I've always wanted to marry you."

She showed me her peach-sweet smile. It was dark in the room, and I couldn't see it, but I could feel it.

She said, "Can we get married in Philadelphia?"

"Philadelphia, a cornfield, a gold mine, an outhouse. It don't matter to me. But shouldn't Scarlett be there when we get hitched?"

"No. It'll be fun to elope. Don't you think?"

"I do."

"How about you save those two words for the wedding ceremony!"

CHAPTER 32

WE SET THE date for Saturday mornin', April 15, the day before Easter.

We'll be in Philadelphia by then, and it'll give us at least a day to rest after our long journey. We'll get married on the courthouse steps and spend the day sightseein'. That evenin' might be a good time to surprise her with a stage show at the Walnut Street Theater, though I might hold back the fact it was Penelope's idea.

Our departure is delayed due to politicians makin' long-winded speeches at the train station. From their version of events you'd think *they* won the war 'stead of the troops and generals!

When the whistle blows and the conductor yells, "All aboard!" I'm stunned to see Enorma standin' by the train to wish us a safe journey. I raise an eyebrow over her and Gentry sharin' a hug. After that, she gives *me* a quick hug and says, "Thanks for everything, Emmett. I'm sorry for the trouble I caused. Have a safe trip. I'll see you in a few weeks."

I climb on board and say, "Goodbye, Enorma."

She waves, then me and Gentry find our seats and wait for the train to take off.

I say, "She seemed in a better mood just now."

"Sometimes a good cry works wonders."

"Were you surprised to see her here?"

"Not really. She asked last night if it would be okay."

"I wonder what she'll decide to do."

"We'll find out soon enough. Why are you grinning at me like that?"

"Your whole face is covered in soot. Not to mention your hair and clothes."

"I can't be as sooty as you!"

"Wanna bet?"

"No. I want to *hide*!"

"They should a' told us about the cinders and soot."

"Who?"

"The Philadelphians."

"You never rode a train before?"

"Nope."

"Well you're on one now!"

"How fast you reckon it'll go?"

The man across the aisle must a' heard our conversation, 'cause he says, "She'll do more than thirty miles an hour."

"Amazin'," I say. "It takes me half a day to travel thirty miles on my horse."

175

"Mind if I ask you a question?" he says.

"Go ahead."

"That gal on the platform."

"What about her?"

"Is she related to you?"

"Yes. She's my daughter. Why do you ask?"

"Oh. Uh...no reason. Enjoy your trip."

"You too."

Gentry says nothin' till the train starts movin'. By then it's huffin' and puffin' and makin' more noise than a mule stuck in a well. When she's positive the man across the aisle can't hear our conversation she says, "Enorma's your *daughter?*"

"I just get tired of dealin' with it, the way men always want to know about Enorma."

"Imagine how *she* feels."

"Sounds like you and her have made up."

"I've tried, Emmett, believe me. But every time I forgive her, she does something to vex me."

"Well, that ought to be past us now."

"You think? Check your coat pocket."

"Why?"

"I might be wrong, but I think she passed you a note when she hugged you."

"I doubt that."

"Let's make sure."

I put my hand in my pocket and pull out a piece of paper.

"I'll be damned," I say.

I hand her the note. She reads it, shakin' her head the whole time. When she's done, she says, "That's a hard girl to like."

"What's it say?"

"I can't believe she lied about her writing skills."

"What do you mean?"

"She told me she could barely read or write. This is a well-written note, with perfect spelling."

"What's it say?"

She reads:

"*Dear Emmett,*

I'm sorry for all the trouble I caused, but as a woman in love, my feelings for you run deep. I'd like to point out I'm only a few years younger than Miss Gentry, and don't mean to disparage her by saying she's got a lot of wear and tear on her private area from five years of hard whoring.

In the event you think it might be a pleasant change to be with a woman no other man has laid eyes on, or taken to bed, I stand ready to serve your needs. I expect it must be hard on you to know that in any room you enter, you could fling a cat and hit a man who's had carnal knowledge of your child's mother.

In making my case for your hand you should be aware I'm a much better cook than Gentry, and have more experience running a home. Also, if you choose to be with me you won't be saddled with having to raise Scarlett, unless that's your preference. And if so, I'll state the obvious, that she and I are in fact closer in age than she and Gentry, and I would prove a willing playmate to her, as well as a loyal homemaker to you.

Here's a suggestion: Gentry can run your whorehouse, I'll run your home.

Speaking of marriage, I'm told it's her choice you've been living together in sin these past years. If that's true and it suits you to be a married man, feel free to leave Gentry in Philadelphia, and marry me on your way back to Dodge. Unlike Miss Gentry, I'd be honored to be your wife.

Your loving admirer,
Enorma Stitz"

After hearin' what Enorma wrote, all I can think to do is take a deep breath. After that's done, I've got no other plan.

Gentry says, "I wonder if train conductors can perform marriages."

"Why?"

"Because I feel like I can't marry you fast enough! Seems every woman in the world has suddenly developed feelings for you. And I fear what might happen when we get to

Philadelphia, where you're considered the hero of the western plains. Women will probably be swooning left and right."

"You're bein' silly."

"I should've married you years ago."

"Well, we'll make up for that on Saturday."

"I should've told her we were getting married."

"She'll know soon enough. I'm proud of you, by the way."

"For what?"

"Not losin' your temper. That was a harsh letter."

"It would be harsher if we weren't on our way to get married."

"I'm glad you read it instead of me. I wouldn't a' been able to read half them words."

"She's a gifted letter-writer for fourteen."

"Maybe she could get a job writin' letters for people who can't read or write."

She thinks a moment. "Why, that's a *wonderful* idea, Emmett!"

"It is?"

"*I* think so. But you know what worries me about all this?"

"What's that?"

"How bad we are as parents."

"Who, you and me?"

"Uh huh."

"Why do you say that?"

"Enorma's only fourteen."

"So?"

"She's technically still a child."

"She don't *look* like a child."

"And you're the one who'd know."

"Sorry."

"Still, I hate to think if Scarlett acts out someday you might shoot her."

"Well..."

"Seriously, Emmett. Was that the only solution available for dealing with a child? To *shoot* her?"

I notice the man in the aisle is starin' at us with a gapin' mouth. Gentry notices it too. She lowers her voice and says, "I'm no better. I gave her some money and told her to go find a whorehouse. Left her alone in a strange city for three or four weeks."

"Like you said, she was plannin' to stay on her own in Philadelphia anyway."

"I know. But I'd like to think I'm a better parent than that."

"We're both better than our parents were. And better than Enorma's."

"Better than Harlan, at least."

"Better than Mary, too. When I told her about my plan to take Enorma to Philadelphia, she said if Enorma didn't want to come back I shouldn't force her."

Gentry shakes her head. "Harlan was making eyes at her, and Mary was jealous. Still, I shouldn't have abandoned her and you shouldn't have shot her."

"Maybe not. But she shouldn't a' done the things she did, neither."

"To which I'd respond she's only fourteen."

"She don't *look* fourteen," I say.

"That's a point you've established and continue to make."

"What should we do? Go back and get her?"

"Yes."

"Really?"

"In three weeks. After we're married. In the meantime, let's promise to become better parents. I'll promise never to abandon Scarlett if you promise not to shoot her."

"What if she acts up?"

"Spank her."

"And Enorma? How should I have handled that situation?"

"Maybe you should have spanked her, as well."

"Turnin' her over my knee didn't seem appropriate, since she was butt-naked."

"Good point. Know what?"

"What?"

"You made the right decision, shooting Enorma. But don't shoot Scarlett, okay?"

"Okay."

CHAPTER 33

THE TRIP TO Philadelphia took four days and six trains.

Train travel is ten times more comfortable than ridin' in a stage coach, which is to say it's God-awful. It was hot, so they kept the windows open most of the way, which meant the cinders and soot were constantly flyin' through the windows. We met some coal miners in Pittsburgh who said ridin' the train was worse than workin' the mines, 'cause the cinders are comin' at you thirty miles an hour! Gentry spent most of the time under a blanket, tryin' to keep from coughin'. We were so tired and uncomfortable we decided to spend a night in Indianapolis, and another in Pittsburgh.

On Friday afternoon we arrive at the Broad Street Station, in Philadelphia. Our buggy driver says we're ten minutes from the Pickering Hotel, which he claims is the finest in the city.

"Where's the courthouse?" I ask.

"Five minutes past the hotel."

Gentry says, "Let's do it, Emmett!"

"Huh?"

"Let's get married right now!"

"You sure?"

"Positive. I know we're covered in soot, but I'd rather check into the hotel a married woman, give you a wonderful wedding night, and sleep in tomorrow morning."

The driver hears all this and says, "Miss? They don't perform weddings at the courthouse."

"They don't?"

Seein' Gentry about to lose her smile, I say, "How about a Justice of the Peace?"

The driver points to a house less than fifty feet away.

Gentry's smile returns.

"Can you take us there and wait?"

"I'll have to charge you extra."

"No problem."

When we get there I say, "You're holdin' all our luggage. I hope I can trust you."

He says, "You're holding a rifle and carrying a side arm. I'd be a fool to cross you."

"What's your name?"

"Chadwick Gates."

"Nice to meet you. I'm Emmett Love."

"Of course you are. And I'm the King of England."

"The what?"

"You said you're Emmett Love. If that's true, I must be the King of England."

Gentry smiles. "They were right. You're famous here."

I look at this feller who claims to be the King of England if I'm me, and say, "Guess you're gonna have to unload the luggage, and carry it inside so I can keep an eye on it, then load it up after the ceremony."

"I'll do nothing of the sort."

I produce my side arm in his face before he has time to blink.

He shrieks like a boiled owl and drops to his knees and begs my forgiveness. I lift him up and explain I don't want his forgiveness, I just want to get married.

"You're Gentry!" he says.

"You've heard of me?"

"The Lily of the Plains? Of course! It's just that—"

"What?"

"I had no idea you folks were real. I thought it was just stories."

"How do you know them stories are true?" I ask.

"If I doubted them before I can't doubt them now. Not after seeing you draw your pistol. I'd be honored to stand for you at the ceremony if you like."

"If you're gonna be my best man, who'll watch our bags?"

"They'll have someone in the building who can guard the coach."

"Then let's do it."

I'd like to say the ceremony is special, but it's just words spoken by a man we never met, and an organ song played by a grim-faced woman after we speak our vows. What's special is the kiss we share. It's the first time I kissed a married woman who weren't a widow.

And I like it.

Afterward, we check into the Pickering and find it every bit as nice as Chadwick said it would be. A man in a funny-lookin' outfit takes our bags up to our room and opens a door we think is a closet, but turns out to have a bathtub in it!

Gentry fairly swoons!

She says, "Just think: if our room in Kansas City had its own bathtub, you wouldn't have had to shoot Enorma!"

The man says he can send for a bath mistress to prepare Gentry's bath. Says it will only take forty-five minutes to get the water ready.

We take him up on his offer and ask about gettin' our sooty clothes cleaned. He says he'll take 'em outside and beat 'em with a stick. I tell him that sounds like fun and ask if I can join him. He laughs like I'm kiddin', but I weren't.

When he leaves, Gentry grins and says, "Bath mistress? Oh, my!"

By the time Gentry's finished her bath, my suit's clean enough to wear to dinner. We enjoy our first meal as a married couple in the hotel restaurant just off the lobby. Gentry calls the food sublime, but even if it was awful I wouldn't a' cared. I'm with Gentry, and we're married, and it's a special evenin', one I'll never forget.

I'll never forget it for three reasons. One: it's our first night together as a married couple. Two: we spend a full hour makin' love. And three: just as our love-makin' ends, we hear people screamin' and yellin' in the lobby downstairs.

"What's happened?" Gentry says.

"I bet the damned war broke out again!"

A 'course it turns out it ain't the war at all, it was a tele-graph message sayin' President Lincoln had been shot a half-hour ago, in a theater, while attendin' a play.

Instead of fallin' asleep in each other's arms we join fifty other hotel guests in the lobby and wait for updates from the telegraph operator. This goes on hour after hour and we pace the floor like you'd do when a loved one is sick or dyin'. The mood in the lobby is as low as it can be. Women are cryin' and prayin', and men are tryin' to comfort 'em. Me and Gentry's doin' the same.

As the time passes, strangers introduce themselves to each other, tell where they're from, and I'm surprised how many have a warm-hearted story to tell about the president.

At first the reports are generally positive. The best news is the president was still alive when the top doctors arrived to treat him a while ago.

"If anyone can pull him through, it's these men," some-one says.

After five hours I talk Gentry into goin' to bed with a promise to wake her if something changes. I tuck her in, hold her close as she cries one last time before fallin' asleep. As I head back to the lobby I'm aware that for the rest of our lives we'll remember our weddin' day as the day President Lincoln got shot. Worse, it happened at the very moment we were consummatin' our marriage. A 'course we didn't know Mr. Lincoln was getting' shot at the time, or we would've been more respectful.

It's a long night for those of us still in the lobby. Every few minutes a new message comes in, and every time it does, we hold our breaths and hope for the best, while bracin' for the worst. But each message turns out to be a re-hash of the ones we've heard before.

At 4:50 a.m. the telegraph operator reads a new one:

"The surgeon general has concluded President Lincoln has suffered a mortal wound and is not expected to survive the night."

The whole lobby bursts into tears. Strangers hug strangers. Men cry unashamed, crushed from the weight of their exhausted emotions. I think about wakin' Gentry to tell her the bad news, but decide she's better off gettin' some rest. If he's truly about to die it won't matter much if I wait till he does. No sense in both of us bein' exhausted.

As the hours go by the messages become progressively grim:

"The first lady, consumed by grief and shock, receives comfort from her eldest son, Robert, in the room adjoining her fallen husband."

"The president continues to fight for his life, but his closest friends—having maintained a vigil throughout the night—say the end is near."

At 8:15 a.m. he reads:

"Vice President Andrew Johnson has confirmed President Abraham Lincoln was pronounced dead at 7:22 a.m. He was shot last night, on Good Friday, while attending a

performance of Our American Cousin at Ford's Theater..."

There's more bein' read about the details, but I can't bear to hear it, 'cause no man could want to spend his weddin' night amid the heavy sadness of heartbroken strangers a minute longer than necessary. The men and women I leave behind in the lobby continue staring blankly at the telegraph machine, as if frozen in time.

Not me.

At this point the details of the shootin' don't make much difference to me. I figure it'll take days to sort out what happened, how it happened, and why.

I turn and trudge back up the stairs knowin' the only comfort to be had on this awful mornin' will be found in my true love's arms. With each step bringin' me closer to her, I say a prayer for the president, and thank the universe that Gentry's my wife, and she's alive, and we're together.

CHAPTER 34

THE ORIGINAL PLAN had been for me and Gentry to set up camp in the hotel lobby Sunday mornin' to meet more than twenty families who wanted to learn what livin' in the west was really like.

At eight a.m. we get the hotel to set aside an area large enough to accommodate the entire crowd, but no one shows up till late afternoon due to the church services takin' place throughout the city to honor the president's life and accomplishments.

When the people show up it's all at once. We meet the Grahams, the Smalleys, the Townsends, Tramonts, Raineys and Ragdales and Spiffles and Spiders.

There ain't no Spiders. I made that up.

There are Gibsons, Singers, Chaffees, and Butts.

I didn't make up the Butts. There truly is an Able and Bertha Butt.

There are more, but I can't remember 'em all. While I field questions from the men, Gentry's busy with the women, writin' down every name and address, includin' the kids. She plans to set up a regular correspondence to try to talk 'em into movin' to Dodge. She even plans to get the women and children of Dodge to write letters to the folks we meet, which I think is a great idea.

The strange thing is I've been talkin' to the men for almost an hour and so far the only thing they want to ask me about is the men I've shot, how the shootin' took place, and what's it like to stare a man down on a street before you shoot him. The real questions that matter come from the women. They want me to verify how the Homestead Act works, and I tell 'em.

"What about the railroad?" someone says.

"We don't have a railroad yet, but it's comin'. Within three years Dodge will have a train station and depot, and regular service to all points east and west."

Someone—a smart ass named Harold Chaffee—says, "Can you guarantee that?"

"Nope. But it's my sincere belief."

"You expect us to move our families to Kansas based on your hopes for securing rail service?"

"Nope. You can move to Dodge or not move to Dodge, as you see fit. But them who do will have rail service in three years if I have to lay it myself."

Chaffee snorts, "With all your legendary accomplishments duly chronicled, would you have us believe that laying railroad track has somehow been overlooked? You're either the most talented man on earth or the world's greatest storyteller."

Part of me wants to shoot him in the foot. The rest of me wants to knock his ass so far into next week he'll see Sunday on both ends. Gentry senses this, and puts her hand on my arm.

I take a deep breath and patiently explain to Chaffee that Burt Bagger left Dodge City and moved to Philadelphia without knowin' I got captured by the Union Army. He never heard they put me to work buildin' the railroad for the troops.

"It weren't pleasant work to perform day in and day out with rags on my body and chains on my ankles while tryin' to subsist on prison food, but if you require a display of me drivin' a railroad spike into a cross tie, I'll be glad to demonstrate my form."

"No need to assemble all that equipment," Chaffee says. "If you were in leg irons as you claim, It would be easy enough to show your scars."

"I wouldn't want to offend the ladies."

"It's just your ankles, sheriff. I'm sure they'll be fine."

I notice everyone's lookin' at me, so I stand, pull up my pants legs and say, "These are the scars from the shackles I wore all them months. I know they ain't pretty to look at. I'm sorry."

Some of the women gasp, but all regard my wounds with sadness and pity. Then I say, "To be honest, my job was more about sledge hammerin' the rocks into gravel to set the cross ties, but every few days one of the linemen would die, and I'd take his place and drive spikes till the next poor soul was captured."

By now the women have turned around to glare at Chaffee. They keep glarin' till he can't stand it anymore. He finally gets up and walks out of the room, draggin' his wife and kids behind him. I say, "Gentry, you might want to cross Mr. Chaffee's name off your pen pal list."

With that behind us the women ask about the school, church, and social events like town functions and celebrations. They ask what type of stores we have, and what the weather's like, and if we have problems with the Indians.

Everyone wants to know about Colorado, and Gentry has to put her hand on my arm several times to keep me from losin' my temper as I explain the difference between rocky soil and bottomland, and the practicality of havin' food to eat in the winter.

Gentry reads the letters written by the Philadelphians who have already moved to Dodge, and everyone has a comment to make about our new friends, who are, of course, *their* friends and relatives.

They all want to see a demonstration of my quick draw, which I'm asked to repeat numerous times. I also have to tell with great detail the story of how I killed Sam Hartmann and nearly got done in by the notorious Bose Rennick moments later. A' course the kids all want to hear stories of Rudy the Bear, and I let Gentry answer most of them questions. By the time she's through, they're howlin' with laughter at her stories of how Rudy got stung by the honey bees, and how he loves to play tag, and how he's the real hero of my Bose Rennick story.

Over the next four days various members of all these families trickle into the lobby time and again to ask additional questions and get further reassurance that Dodge is a worthy place to settle down. A' course, these families told other families that the famous Emmett and Gentry Love— recently married—are holdin' court in the lobby of the Pickering Hotel. By Friday afternoon Gentry's accumulated more than a hundred and seventy names of men, women, and children from forty-eight different families who are considerin' movin' to Dodge over the next few years.

By Friday night we're all talked out, and plan some quiet time for a romantic dinner, our first since the weddin'.

But that only lasts ten minutes.

Before we have time to order, Gentry looks up past my shoulder and all the color drains from her face.

CHAPTER 35

"WHAT'S WRONG?"

"It's George!"

"Who?"

"The man Scarlett drew in the picture. Remember?"

I do. and the man approachin' our table is the spittin' image of the man Scarlett identified as George. She drew him perfectly, from his long curly hair to his mustache, wide-brimmed hat, and sissy-lookin' scarf.

He says, "Do I have the honor of addressing Sheriff Emmett Love, of Dodge City, Kansas?"

"You do."

"A pleasure to meet you sir." He tips his hat to Gentry and says, "I'm Major General George Armstrong Custer. Would it be too great an imposition to sit with you a few minutes?"

I look at Gentry.

"I'll be brief," he says."

Gentry motions him to take a seat.

I say, "I never met a general before."

He frowns. "Technically you're not meeting one now. I'm afraid I embellished my rank just now. I was Brevit Major General during the war."

"What's that mean?"

"Temporary. I need to get used to being a colonel again. Forgive me if I got your attention through false pretense."

"I met a Union colonel once before."

"I trust it was a good experience."

"He stole my horse and put me in chains. What brings you to Philadelphia?"

"The viewing tomorrow. Do you plan to attend?"

"I'm told it ain't till Sunday."

"The public viewing, yes."

"We'd love to attend, but I understand the line could be a mile long."

"Whoever told you that is misinformed. I have it on good authority more than a quarter million people will pass by the president's coffin on Sunday. The line could exceed three miles and take five hours."

"That's a lot of standin' and waitin' in the heat," I say.

"Truly, it is. Which is why I'd like you to be my guests at the private viewing tomorrow night."

Gentry's face lights up. "What time?"

"Ten p.m."

She gives me a hopeful look.

I say, "We wouldn't want to impose..."

"It would be my honor, sir. Do you know where Independence Hall is located?"

"I'm told it's only five minutes away."

"That's correct. If you meet me there at nine-forty, I'll provide your personal escort."

"That's mighty kind of you."

He tips his hat. Then says, "I'm told you're an experienced Indian fighter."

"I've been in a few scrapes."

"What can you tell me about the Cheyenne?"

"They ain't as plentiful as they used to be."

"Thanks to you?" He says, chucklin'.

"I was actually referrin' to the cholera epidemic of 1849. But havin' said that, there's still plenty of Indians to go around."

"So I hear. General Sheridan has offered me command of the Second Division of Cavalry, Military Division of the Southwest."

"That's a helluva title."

He gives me a look. "It's an adequate description of my rank, sir."

I nod, wonderin' if he's angry or just bein' precise. I wouldn't call him pompous, but he's certainly confident, and a bit of a dandy. I doubt the southwestern troops will enjoy bein' ordered around by an easterner wearin' dandy duds.

"As to the Cheyenne," I say, "I've found them to be a peace-lovin' people who are extremely family-oriented."

His ears perk up. "What do you mean, 'family-oriented?'"

"Of all the tribes I've encountered, Cheyenne warriors place the highest value on their elders, wives, and children."

"By 'highest value' you mean what, exactly?"

"A Cheyenne warrior would never put a tribe member in harm's way. They're an extremely devoted people."

"I admire them," Custer says. "I'm told they're fierce fighters."

"They can be. And when provoked, they're quick to unite with other tribes."

"Interesting."

Custer spends a few minutes talking about President Lincoln, and the war, and shares some details of Lee's surrender at Appomattox, which he personally attended. Gentry makes a comment about the enormous loss of life caused by the war, and Custer points out more men were killed by disease than fightin'. If that's meant to change Gentry's opinion it don't work.

Custer abruptly stands and says, "I've intruded long enough. Thanks for indulging my questions, and congratulations on your recent marriage. I look forward to seeing you tomorrow night."

After he leaves, Gentry says, "I never saw a man dress like that."

"How much time do you think he spends waxin' his mustache?"

"Who cares? Oh, oh. Now I feel bad."

"Why?"

She points to the waiter headin' toward us with a bottle of champagne. He sets it on the table with a flourish and says, "Compliments of General Custer."

I don't correct him. I figure Colonel Custer don't mind bein' thought a general.

"What do you think it means?" Gentry says.

"The champagne?"

"No. I mean the fact that Scarlett drew his likeness weeks ago without ever having seen him."

"Not only that, but she knew his name was George."

We're quiet till Gentry says, "Whatever it means, I miss her. I want to go home."

"It's settled," I say.

"Really?"

"Yes. We'll take this bottle of champagne upstairs to our room. You'll take off your clothes and climb in the tub and I'll pour it all over you. Then you can say you've had your champagne bath."

"That's very thoughtful of you, but I thought we were talking about going home."

"We'll go home first thing Sunday mornin'."

"*Really?* That's a week earlier than we planned!"

"It was the champagne bath that sealed the deal."

"The kind of bath you're talking about sounds chilly."

"I'll warm you up right after.

She smiles. "Thank you, Emmett."

"My pleasure," I say, tippin' my hat.

CHAPTER 36

GENTRY AND ME are in awe.

We're in what Custer calls the "hallowed halls" of the East Wing of Independence Hall, where the Declaration of Independence was signed less than ninety years ago. Viewing is by invitation only, and most who were invited personally knew the president. Colonel Custer has powerful friends here, and is courteous enough to introduce us around.

Bein' here's the most solemn occasion I ever attended, or ever will. We're actually standin' beside the open casket, lookin' at our president's face and body. It don't seem right starin' at him like this. It seems like the worst possible invasion of privacy, one I wouldn't tolerate if he was my relative. But everyone who knew him swears this is how he wanted it, since he was such a man of the people.

Gentry can't control her emotions. Havin' recently become an enthusiastic reader of books and newspapers, she knew much more about the man and his deeds than me. But even for me it's hard to be in the presence of such a beloved, powerful man, havin' to see him like this, struck down in his prime, before he had a chance to rebuild the country.

After they usher us away from the casket we thank Colonel Custer for invitin' us here tonight, and for the bottle of champagne he gave us last night.

"I hope you found it a pleasurable vintage," he says.

I give Gentry a wink and say, "Pleasurable is the exact word I'd use to describe it."

The next mornin' we board the train to Pittsburgh, where we plan to take a steamboat ride to Cincinnati, just to say we did. The attendant informs us the trip will take twice as long as usual, since the railroad has added four extra cars and will make a dozen unscheduled stops to accommodate the soldiers heading back to their homes in central and western Pennsylvania.

He weren't lyin'. It takes us two days and nights to get to Pittsburgh! When we get there Gentry says, "Colonel Custer was right about the viewing line yesterday."

She's readin' a newspaper while waitin' on a carriage to take us to the steamship dock.

"What's it say?"

"Two lines of people stretched more than three miles long. Some waited up to five hours to see the president. Some fainted, some got their clothes ripped, and one lady sustained a broken arm."

"Mr. Lincoln couldn't have wanted *that*," I say.

When we get to the steamship dock they tell us all the ships have been dispatched to New Orleans, Vicksburg, and Memphis, to pick up soldiers. The ticket man notes Gentry's disappointment and says, "Ma'am, if you've got your heart set on a steamship ride, you could take the train to Cincinnati and catch an eastbound steamship to Maysville. From there you could take a train back to Cincinnati."

We thank him for the information and decide to do it.

"When you get to the dock in Cincinnati, ask for Mr. Eggman. He oversees several steamships, including the *Sultana*."

CHAPTER 37

"IT WOULD BE an honor to have Sheriff Love and his new bride on one of our sternwheelers!" Eggman gushes. "I hope you'll allow me to have a photographer record the event for posterity."

I look at the approachin' steamship. "Is that the one we'd be ridin'?"

"It is."

"Nice ship."

"It's the *Excelsior*. While not as nice as the *Sultana*, I think you'll be more than pleased. General boarding's in an hour, so perhaps we can get you positioned for a photograph when the troops disembark."

I point at the throng of war prisoners waitin' to board. "Are all them troops gonna board this ship?"

"They are."

"And some who are on board will stay?"

"Yes. Most will continue all the way to Pittsburgh. Why do you ask?"

"I appreciate your hospitality, but I reckon we won't be ridin' with you today."

Gentry's face falls. So does Mr Eggman's. He says, "Why not?"

"Too many men. Not enough boat."

Eggman chuckles. "You have steamship experience, do you?"

"Nope. But I know how many men can ride a stagecoach."

"And how many's that?"

"Depends on the horses and terrain to be covered. But I'd never put forty men on a stagecoach just because there's enough room for 'em to fit."

"There's a huge difference between a steamship and a stage coach. Whereas horses *pull* a stagecoach, the steamboat's engines push it over the water. The result is a smooth glide."

He winks at Gentry, which annoys me, 'cause now she's givin' me a hopeful look. I scowl and say, "I ain't a stranger to rivers. I've poled a few rafts in my time, and a keelboat, too. Durin' them times the lessons came quick, and weren't forgivin'."

"Tell me, Mr. Love. What did you learn while *poling* the rivers?"

"I learned that polin' upstream's a damn sight harder than floatin' downstream. I also learned the current's relentless. If you're up against it, you can't take a break, 'cause if you do, you'll fall behind. You can pole for an hour, take a five minute rest and wind up further behind than you were an hour ago."

He grins. "You're making an excellent case for why we use steamships today instead of keel boats."

"Steam or keel, there's a breakin' point."

Eggman frowns. "Trying to compare a group of men poling a keelboat to a steamship is like comparing ants to Indians."

"Enough ants can kill a man."

He takes a deep breath. "Would it be fair to say you say you've shared your complete knowledge of rivers with me?"

"Nope," I say. "I learned one other thing."

"What's that?"

"I've rafted without a poll."

"You have."

"Yup."

"And what did you take from that experience?"

"Too many men on board will sink a raft."

"It might interest you to know *The Sultana* left Vicksburg yesterday carrying twenty three hundred passengers. It's already made three stops without incident. The ship coming in right now will only be transporting six hundred."

"It's still too many. I hope the undertakers have a large stock of pine."

Eggman gives me the kind of smile a parent gives a child who's worried about the bogeyman. Then turns to Gentry and says, "Do you share your husband's views on the dangers of river travel?"

"I trust Emmett to know what's right for us."

"What a delightful answer!" he says. "You're a lucky man, Mr. Love."

"I am, indeed."

He tips his hat to Gentry. "Ma'am."

She nods. "Nice to meet you." As he turns to leave she says, "Mr. Eggman?"

"Yes?"

"If my husband tells you a piss ant can pull a buckboard, you'd best saddle him up."

After he leaves she says, "Are you sure it's dangerous, Emmett? Mr. Eggman seems so confident, and we've come so far to get to this point. It almost seems like destiny, since we arrived just moments before the next one's about to board."

"I'm stickin' to my guns, Gentry. That's too many passengers. It's dangerous."

She nods her head and says, "Okay then, let's head home."

"Gentry?"

"Yes?"

"Thanks for backin' me up with Mr. Eggman. I know you're disappointed."

"You're my husband. It's my job to back you up."

"And it's my job to protect you."

"I know, Emmett. And I love you for worrying about my safety. I know it wasn't easy telling me no. So let's put all this behind us and hurry home to see Scarlett. We can save the steamship experience for another day, and have it to look forward to."

"By then maybe they'll have water closets in the hotels."

She smiles. "Maybe so."

When our train pulls into Saint Louis Friday mornin', Gentry buys a newspaper and reads it while we wait for the passengers to load. After a while she says, "Emmett?"

"Yes?"

"You were wrong about the *Excelsior*."

"It arrived safely?"

"There's nothing in the paper about it sinking."

"Well, I'm not sorry about that. I'd rather be proven wrong than see men lose their lives. I'm sorry I was overcautious."

"Don't be. You were right about the danger."

She angles the paper toward me and points to an article that says the steamship *Sultana* blew up yesterday mornin' and sank north of Memphis, killin' seventeen hundred passengers. The government intends to launch an investigation into why twenty-three hundred passengers were on board a ship that was only certified to carry three hundred seventy-six.

Gentry says, "I think we dodged a bullet."

PART THREE:
A BLAST FROM THE PAST

CHAPTER 38

WHEN WE ARRIVE in Kansas City we head straight to the hotel to check on Enorma...

And find her in the lobby, surrounded by men!

Gentry smiles. "Guess you'll have to wait in line if you're still interested in runnin' off with her."

"I was never interested."

"But you were fascinated with her work ethic."

I shake my head.

Gentry says, "I told you she'd be fine on her own!"

"You did, indeed."

We watch her regale the crowd from a distance, amazed at how she's got 'em all captivated and laughin', and hangin' on her every word.

"Notice her outfit?" Gentry says.

"What about it?"

"I didn't buy it."

"Maybe she bought it with the money you gave her."

"And the jewelry?"

I hadn't seen that. "Wow."

"Wow, indeed!"

After a while Enorma looks up, sees us, and squeals with delight. She calls us over and introduces us as her dearest friends from Dodge City. After a few minutes of small talk, Gentry says, "Oh, by the way, Emmett and I exchanged vows in Philadelphia."

"What type of vows?" Enorma asks.

"Wedding."

Enorma looks at me. "You're married."

"We are."

She asks her fellers to excuse her for the evenin' so she can talk to us about our recent trip. Some of the men are frustrated, some are annoyed, and some have tears in their eyes.

As does Enorma.

One by one they take her hand, kiss it, and say, "Goodbye, Enorma."

CHAPTER 39

WHEN WE GET back to Dodge the whole town turns out to celebrate our arrival.

Gentry and I are thrilled to meet the new Philadelphians who were travelin' to Dodge as we headed east. Both old and new were impressed we met Custer, who they insist is quite the celebrity back east. But they were positively astonished to hear he bought us champagne and invited us to the private viewing of the president's body.

We're pleased to hear Winifred, Amelia, and Penelope have already made their trip to Saint Jo and secured the services of nearly forty carpenters and workers who'll be arriving within days to start the long-overdue construction projects. Though we're dyin' to socialize and hear all the details, what we want most is to spend time with Scarlett.

On this occasion, Scarlett don't seem like an old soul or a twelve-year-old, or a girl who speaks snake. She seems like

211

an ordinary child that's excited to see her parents. When she hears we got married the first thing she wants to see is her mama's ring.

Me and Gentry look at each other and bust out laughin'.

We forgot to shop for one!

Harlan and Mary ask us privately what happened to Enorma. After givin' Harlan a harsh look for lustin' after his stepdaughter, Gentry tells 'em the full story.

The next day I'm in my sheriff's office when the door opens.

It's Penelope.

I give her a broad smile and start to say somethin' about meetin' some a' her friends in Philadelphia when she walks right up to me and slaps my face with all her might.

"How *could* you!" she says.

I rub my cheek. For a city gal she packs a wallop. Before I can ask what's got her so riled, she says, "We spoke *words*!"

That don't make sense. I've spoke words to everyone in Dodge, but few have slapped me for it.

"Foolish me," she says. "I thought we had an understanding."

"About what?" I say.

She looks up at the ceilin', closes her eyes, takes a deep breath. Then lowers her head, and looks me in the eye.

"About *us*!" she says. "You said you understood! And now you've come home married." She pauses. "*Married!*"

She stares at me another minute, then stomps out the door.

Seconds later the door opens again.

I look up, expectin' to see Penelope, but it ain't her. It's Sadie Nickers, and she's grinnin' like a possum eatin' shit off a wire brush.

"I think you just lost one of your admirers," she says.

"What do you mean?"

"I never saw a proper woman so angry. What'd you do, get her pregnant?"

"A' course not. There was just a misunderstandin'."

"Judgin' from that slap mark on your face, I'd say it was your fault."

"It probably was. What can I do for you?"

"I wanted to show you somethin' I took in trade last week from the Dog Soldiers."

"What is it?"

"Stay put. I'll bring it in."

I thought I'd seen it all.

I thought there was nothin' left to see.

But when I saw what Sadie Nickers took in trade I got the biggest shock of my life.

Seriously.

The biggest shock...

Of my life.

CHAPTER 40

IT'S A WOMAN. And Sadie's got a lead line tied to her neck!

She ain't pullin' the line, nor is the woman strugglin'. She's dressed up like an Indian squaw, with a fringed shirt, tall boots, and a leather skirt made from tanned deer hide. Her shirt and skirt are decorated with berry ink, porcupine quills, and wild hog tusks.

Except that she ain't an Indian, she's a white woman.

She appears to be my age, though I know her to be eight years younger.

We stare at each other a full minute, till she finally says, "Emmett? Is that really you?"

She crosses the room and takes me in her arms.

So dumbstruck am I, I'm unable to speak or move a muscle.

Sadie laughs at my expression. "You look like you just saw a ghost!"

I want to respond, but can't form the words.

The woman backs away from me and looks into my eyes as if trying to connect with a dead man.

I finally stammer out the only words that make sense to say.

"I thought you were dead."

"I know."

Sadie says, "I didn't believe her at first, but she seemed so sincere. Now I'm gonna go out on a limb and assume the story she told me is true."

I nod. "It's true. This is my wife, Amy."

Sadie says, "I'd give my left tit to be there when you tell Gentry."

CHAPTER 41

AFTER SADIE LEAVES I try to remove the rope from Amy's neck, but she backs away and says, "Please. Leave it on. It's how I've gotten around for fifteen years."

"I can't just lead you through town like this," I say.

"It will be fine."

I only live a hundred yards from the sheriff's office, but by the time Amy and me reach my front yard, half the town's followin' us.

Gentry, Scarlett, and Rose come out the front door to see what all the fuss is about. Before I get a chance to say anythin', Scarlett hollers, "Can I keep her?"

Amy smiles at Scarlett, then closes her eyes and inhales deeply. A moment later she stands a little straighter.

Scarlett smiles back.

Gentry says, "What's this about? Who *is* this poor woman, and why have you put a rope around her neck?"

I turn and ask the town folks to go on about their business, but none of 'em move so much as a hair. So I threaten 'em with jail time. When *that* don't work I draw my gun and shoot the ground in front of a woman's toe.

That works.

The whole group skedaddles till there's just me, Amy, Gentry, Scarlett, and Rose.

"Who *is* she, Papa?"

"Good question," Gentry says. "And one I've asked already. Emmett? I'd like an answer, and I'd like it now."

I try to think of a better way than to blurt out she's my wife, but nothin' comes to mind.

"She's my long-lost wife," I say, and Gentry falls to the floor in a dead faint.

Over the next hour I explain how Amy and me got married in 1849 when she was fourteen and I was twenty-two, and how some Masikotas attacked the tiny settlement where we lived and killed all the people. In them days the Indians burned all the whites they killed 'cause of the cholera epidemic, so I counted the charred bodies and the total was right for the whole settlement, includin' Amy. Now I figure they must have had a young woman with 'em that they killed to hide the kidnappin'. That's the woman I buried in Amy's grave. The Masikotas were known not to take prisoners, so it never dawned on me Amy could have been alive. Nor have me or Shrug ever heard news of a white woman livin' among the Dog Soldiers.

"Where were you when the town came under attack?" Rose asks.

"Trackin' the band of Comanche that killed my parents."

Gentry says, "In all the time we've been together, how is it you never thought to mention you were married?"

"It pained me to talk about it."

She looks at Amy. "How long had you been married when this happened?"

"Six weeks."

"Was there a child?"

"No."

To me she says, "What are your plans for Amy? Surely you don't expect her to stay *here!*"

I sigh. "She's got no place else to go."

"You can't be serious! Wait. Why is she here in the first place?"

"The Dog Soldiers traded her for some Henry rifles."

Gentry shakes her head, unable to comprehend.

Amy says, "I won't make trouble. I'm a good worker."

Gentry looks at me with pleadin' eyes. "Emmett?"

"She won't be stayin' in our house," I say.

"Why not?" Scarlett says. "I like her."

"Of course you do," Gentry says.

"She can sleep with me!" Scarlett says.

"I'll be more comfortable with the horses," Amy says. "Where do you keep them?"

"In stalls."

"I can sleep there. I'm good with horses."

Gentry says, "You can't sleep in a stall. What would the neighbors think?" She looks at me. "There must be another solution. One that doesn't involve her living under our roof."

"There is. I'll build her a small house."

"Where?"

I was about to say the vacant lot next door to us, but Gentry's look inspires me to say, "On the opposite end of town."

"That's a nice area. Where will she stay till then?"

"I expect she'll be fine in one of the horse stalls. But I can put a pallet in the card emporium and she can sleep beside Rudy, if she don't mind bears."

Amy's eyes grow large.

Apparently she don't like bears.

"One of the horse stalls sounds perfect," Amy says.

That night, when Gentry and me are in bed, she says, "I'm really sorry for the way I acted about Amy. I know she's had a terrible life, and it's not her fault or yours for what happened. But it just seems like everything you do leads to other women that I have to deal with on a daily basis."

"You mean like May Gray?"

"Yes. And our whores."

"What about 'em?"

"They've seen you naked, taking well baths, and always tease me about it. And of course there's Margaret."

"Margaret Stallings?"

"Yes. I never accused you of this, but the gossip around town is she and May Gray were fighting over you before you rescued me from Mr. Wilkins. From what I hear, she kissed you right in the middle of the street, and you let her. And then she kissed you a second time. Then she took you in her house and when you came out an hour later she was the new mayor."

"I can see how that might *appear* improper, but—"

"Did she kiss you?"

"Yes, but it was a happy kiss."

"Aren't all kisses happy?"

"She was excited at findin' the key to my shackles."

"Still, it's another woman. And let's not overlook Penelope."

"Penelope?"

"You've seen the way she looks at you. And when you look at her she sighs hard enough to power a grist mill. She's got some sort of notion in her head about you. And what about this Sadie Nickers character?"

"What about her?"

"She trades guns for women and brings them to you. I mean, is this going to become a regular thing with her?"

"No, a' course not. It were a special case with Amy."

"Which brings us to your long-lost wife, Amy. I suppose I'll be running into her several times a week for the rest of my life."

"I doubt she'll be a problem."

"I expect you're right, but you've got to admit, it's a lot for me to deal with."

"What do you mean?"

"Between old and new Dodge there are what, twenty women?"

"Something like that."

"Why does it seem they're all a threat to our marriage?"

"There ain't no threats to our marriage, Gentry. Everyone in town knows that."

She sighs. "I hope that's true. But Emmett?"

"Yes?"

"Please. No more women, okay? No more surprises. I mean, we're done now, right? There are no other wives or girlfriends, no one else in town that's kissed you or pulled your pecker, or seen you naked, right?"

"Right."

"Say the words."

"No more surprises, Gentry. We're done. All the surprises are behind us now."

A few minutes goes by. Then she says, "I'll probably grow to like Amy."

"You probably will."

"As long as she doesn't entertain ideas of getting back together with you."

"She won't."

"Good. I can deal with it. As long as nothing else comes our way."

"It won't."

"You promise?"

"I do."

CHAPTER 42

THE NEXT MORNIN' a nice young man enters my office and introduces himself as Benjamin Suiters. He says he just came from the land office, where he purchased the lot next to mine and plans to build a beautiful house there.

I'm thrilled to hear the news. For one thing, he seems like a nice young man. For another, I won't have to feel guilty about not givin' the lot to Amy.

"Where are you from, Ben?"

"Saint Jo."

"What type of work do you do?"

"I'm in the lumber business."

The news gets better and better.

He asks if I have any children. I tell him about Scarlett.

"Do you have kids?" I say.

"Not yet, but we plan to. It's early yet. We just got married."

"Me and Gentry just got married a couple weeks ago."

"It's great, isn't it? Marriage, I mean?"

"It is. I can't wait to meet your wife."

"You won't have to. She's right outside."

He opens the door. I watch her walk in.

She smiles warmly.

I say, "Hello, Enorma."

THE END

Oh wait! There's more . . .

Author Note: 1

In the spring of 1865 the Sioux, Cheyenne, Arapaho, and others began attacking settlers and small troop encampments in Nebraska and Kansas. The army responded by sending hundreds of troops to quell the uprisings. For a time the Indians held their own. But that changed as the army gained in size and strength.

Four days after Scartlett Rose celebrated her seventh birthday, Colonel George A. Custer ordered his 7th Cavalry to attack Black Kettle's camp on the Washita River. Although Custer knew Black Kettle's followers were considered friendly, some of his warriors were rumored to have participated with the Dog Soldiers in raids on nearby settlements. Custer's men killed 150 Indians, mostly women and children, and nearly 700 horses and dogs. All the wounded, including women and children, were systematically executed.

During the battle, Black Kettle and his wife were shot in the back and killed as they attempted to escape on horseback.

Former gunslinger and noted sheriff, Emmett Love, never forgave himself for telling Custer how family-oriented the Cheyenne were. He was especially horrified to hear that after massacring Black Kettle's camp, Custer and his men escaped the area by using fifty-three women and children as human shields, a tactic that became routine in fighting the Cheyenne.

In his book, *My Life on the Plains*, Custer wrote: "Indians contemplating a battle, either offensive or defensive, are always anxious to have their women and children removed from all danger."

Although Gentry Love spent her whole life trying to convince her husband that Custer would have learned about the Cheyenne's devotion to family on his own, Emmett went to his grave believing it was the comments he made to Custer, in April of 1865, in Philadelphia, that were directly responsible for the deaths of hundreds of peaceful Indians, predominately women and children.

Author Note: 2

In the summer of 2013, a small portion of a dime novel, circa 1862, was found in New York City, in Central Park, at the site of an urban terrorist attack. Attached to the cover was a note addressed to Donovan Creed, Agency Director, Sensory Resources. There was no signature on the note, just the words: *Because We Can!*

Special Offer from John Locke!

If you like my books, you'll LOVE my mailing list! By joining, you'll receive discounts of up to 67% on future eBooks. Plus, you'll be eligible for amazing contests, drawings, and you'll receive immediate notice when my newest books become available!

Visit my website:
http://www.DonovanCreed.com

John Locke

New York Times Best Selling Author
8th Member of the Kindle Million Sales Club
*(which includes James Patterson, Stieg Larsson,
George R.R. Martin and Lee Child, among others)*

John Locke had 4 of the top 10 eBooks on
Amazon/Kindle at the same time, including #1 and #2!

...Had 6 of the top 20, and 8 books in the
top 43 at the same time!

...Has written 19 books in three years in
four separate genres, all best-sellers!

...Has been published in numerous languages by many of the
world's most prestigious publishing houses!

Donovan Creed Series:

Lethal People
Lethal Experiment
Saving Rachel
Now & Then
Wish List
A Girl Like You
Vegas Moon
The Love You Crave
Maybe
Callie's Last Dance

Emmett Love Series:

Follow the Stone
Don't Poke the Bear
Emmett & Gentry
Goodbye, Enorma

Dani Ripper Series:

Call Me
Promise You Won't Tell?

Dr. Gideon Box Series:

Bad Doctor
Box

Other:

Kill Jill

Non-Fiction:

How I Sold 1 Million eBooks in 5 Months!

Made in the USA
Lexington, KY
06 September 2013